Upon a Nation's Honour

A Sherlock Holmes Adventure

John Sutton

Paperback ISBN 978-1-78705-236-9
ePub ISBN 978-1-78705-237-6
PDF ISBN 978-1-78705-238-3

Published in the UK by MX Publishing
335 Princess Park Manor, Royal Drive,
London, N11 3GX
www.mxpublishing.co.uk

Cover design by Brian Belanger

Chapter One

Naval Dockyard, Portsmouth, October 1906

The dense evening sea fog settled like a grey shroud over the naval dockyard, converting the bright electric lighting into pale glimmers that bisected the dismal gloom.

The massive ship rested silently within the huge dock. Her superstructure gleamed beneath the clammy embrace of the heavy fog. Her huge hull dwarfed the dock in which she rested quietly. Her superstructure rose like a pyramid behind her frontal, armoured turrets sprouting barrels of her huge 12 inch cannons, their black, cavernous snouts, promising imminent and indefensible destruction to any, who might defy her absolute power.

She had been designed and constructed as the ultimate weapon of the sea and her introduction into the British Navy had at a single act -- rendered the battleships of the rest of the world obsolete.

High upon the steel gangway that overlooked the ship's awful might, the naval sentry shivered, then assured himself that this involuntary action was occasioned by the clammy cold that infested the huge building in which the vessel lay.

Sidney Shilton had enlisted in His Majesty's Royal Navy some three years earlier.

It had not been a decision taken lightly. It was a statement of his desire to improve his then foreseeable life, away from his expected future. Sidney had been born a son of a coal miner and having experienced the terrible conditions of those obliged to accept this arduous, dangerous and poorly paid occupation, had decided to break with the "miner- son" tradition.

In the Royal Navy -- Sidney had discovered comradeship and the ability for unbelievable advancement, unavailable in civilian life. Sidney loved his new life and fortune appeared to favour him. Taller than the average sailor at that time, Sidney's liking for female company, ensured him a collection of willing ladies, within any station that he was placed. Life couldn't be better for Sidney.

Even his selection as naval sentry to stand guard over the mighty warship bothered him little. His superiors must trust him above others to place him in this prestigious situation. Suddenly, his whole body was overcome with a feeling of warmth and well being. His duty finished at 0600 hrs. tomorrow, and Sally had at last, agreed to walk out with him as "his girl."

For a brief moment, his preoccupation with the possibilities of the forthcoming evening dulled his normally alert senses and thus, with a sense of shock, he suddenly felt the hard hand clamp over his mouth and then, the agonising bite of the blade that severed his wind pipe and aorta.

He wanted to say something -- anything, yet the lack of air and the torrent of blood prevented this. As his dying body slowly slumped to the hard, glistening steel of the gangway, his departing senses briefly grappled with life then sank into the black pit of eternity.

Berlin, Germany, February 1906

The soft, milky blue orbs stared blankly into the roaring logs of the huge fire that bathed the otherwise dark room in a flickering canopy of light.
A man in his late fifties slumped unmoving within the confines of the leather, fireside chair. The deep crimson of the silk smoking jacket appeared crumpled by the man's position and the twin ends of a hastily unravelled dinner tie, hung as loose fronds over the pristine white shirt that evidenced the onset of a paunch. Below the crimson cummerbund, the black clad right leg thrust straight and motionless towards the blazing fire. The other bent at an angle, allowing the foot to rest upon the heavy piled carpet of the room. The figure's left hand, clasping a near empty balloon of brandy, rested motionless upon the corresponding arm of the chair. It was only the continual drumming of the left leg upon the floor that indicated any sign of life from the man before the large fire.

Colonel Sebastian Moran, formerly of Her Imperial Majesty's forces then paid assassin of the late Professor Moriarty, hounded by the British authorities and forced to flee his country of birth -- now sat within a large house upon the outskirts of Berlin, Germany.
Moran was deliberating upon the fortunes of his existence when, a slight tap was heard from a door to

3

the side of the room. The hand clutching the glass moved and from within the chair a disgruntled voice spoke.

"Ja?"

The door opened, emitting a bright shard of electrical light from the areas without the room.

"Herr Oberst, General von Schiffert is here," said a voice in near perfect English.

"Ask the General to come in Karl," instructed Moran.

"May I turn on the electric lights, Herr Oberst?" enquired the other.

"Yes!"

Suddenly the room became illuminated, evidencing the heavy tapestries and rich decor associated with 19th. century German furnishings.

General von Schiffert walked into the room and stood before Moran. He bowed politely and spoke.

"Oberst Moran, Ich denke das die Zeit fur eines kleines gesproch hat gekommen."

Moran rose slowly from his chair and regarded the other.

"Bitte, Herr General, he began, "Ich spreche nicht gut Deutsch. Wollen sie auf Englische sprechen?"

The general smiled softly. "Of course," he replied in perfect English. "Please forgive me. I thought that the last year within my country, might have afforded you a greater understanding of our language."

Moran placed his glass of brandy upon the small table that stood close and smiled a corresponding response.

"Then you must forgive my tardiness, Herr General," he said. "During my time in your country I have had little opportunity to leave this house and meet with other Germans. My staff, such as you have provided, normally converse with me in my own language although Karl, upon my insistence, attempts to teach me your tongue."

Von Schiffert inclined his head politely. "I understand perfectly," he began. "I have been fortunate enough, as a member of the Kaiser's Sichersheitdienst, to have been afforded to opportunity to learn several languages."

At these words, Moran stiffened perceptibly.

"Sicherheitsdienst?"

"Secret Service," replied von Schiffert.

"Germany possesses a Secret Service?" asked Moran to which the other nodded.

"A new country, struggling to assert itself within larger countries envious of its potential power and ambitions, requires intelligence," he stated. "Now! If I may sit down?" Moran, realising his faux pas, hurriedly indicated another chair that rested opposite to the one in which he had been sitting. "Please, Herr General." he expostulated. "Forgive my rudeness."

Von Schiffert settled himself within the proffered chair.

"Perhaps some refreshment," continued Moran. "A little supper?" Von Schiffert shook his head.

"I have eaten already at my club," he remarked. "However, a glass of brandy would be most appreciated."

Moran called out, "Karl!"

The door opened again, and the orderly entered. "Ya!

Herr Oberst?"

"Zwei grossen Brandiies, schnell!" ordered Moran.

"Jawohl! Herr Oberst!" replied the other and disappeared from the room.

"You are learning something," mused von Schiffert. "When you indicated the figure of two, you used your thumb and the first finger. An Englishman would employ the first and second fingers. A definite give-away, if you are attempting to impersonate a European of whatever nationality. I note that you maybe learning some of our ways."

For a few moments while they awaited the delivery of their drinks, the men talked innocently upon such subjects as, the beauty of the Unter den Linden in spring and, the jollity of the Tiergarten with its cosmopolitan atmosphere.

However, following the reappearance of Karl with the refreshment and his final disappearance behind the closed door, the atmosphere of the room became far more serious.

"Are you enjoying your stay in my country?" enquired von Schiffert.

"Germany has proved a most welcoming state," replied Moran. "Every wish and desire has been most attended to. Such a change from the reception I was used to in my country of birth."

Von Schiffert nodded contentedly. "For this, I may only say that Germany will always welcome those who feel obliged to shall I say, change their national allegiance." he murmured

He regarded Moran and his face became fixed. "I may assume that this fact has occurred?" he enquired.

Moran had little problem in his reply. "Be assured, Herr von Schiffert that any loyalty that I may have formerly shown to my country of birth, no longer exists. The English have rewarded me with nothing but rejection and hatred. That is why I travelled to Germany, where shall I say, my talents may be more appreciated." Von Schiffert smiled wickedly.

"Good! -- then I assume that a small request to you upon my government's behalf that might result in some injury to England would cause you little consternation?"

Moran nodded. "I have little but utter hatred for a country that has so churlishly abandoned me and more to the point, would surely hang me, if I remained within their jurisdiction," he stated. "Pray tell me -- how may I be of service?"

"How far are you prepared to go to damage your previous country?" asked von Schiffert.

"To whatever lengths you wish me to travel," replied Moran.

"Good!" exclaimed von Schiffert, "That is all I wish to determine. Now I will tell you what I need you to do." Von Schiffert paused and took a sip of his brandy before continuing.

"Be assured, colonel Moran that, should you accept my commission and waiver in any way, then the luxury you have enjoyed within my country will cease and you will immediately be repatriated to the country toward which you bear so much hatred. I do not have to illustrate what will then become of you, should this unhappy event occur."

Moran appeared unaffected. "Then tell me what you wish me to do?" he said.

Von Schiffert took another gulp at his brandy, "Quite simply, Colonel Moran," he said softly. "You are to head a team of men that I shall personally recruit, travel to England and obtain a piece of equipment that may prove vital to our navy's performance in any future conflict with the country that you, so obviously despise. Would you be willing to undertake such an exercise?"

For a few moments, Moran stroked his throat as if feeling the knot of the hangman's rope.

"You make it impossible for me to refuse," he said softly.

Warehouse, Albert Smith & Co, Portsmouth, October 1906

Albert Smith had arrived in Portsmouth late in 1898, acquired a reasonably lengthy lease on a small warehouse and commenced business as a wholesale grocer.

Within his first two years, Albert's business had grown to such an extent that, by 1900, he purchased the freehold to a large building and transferred his stock into more accommodatable premises.

It must be said that, although Albert's personal business acumen contributed in no small way to the success of the business, most of the larger orders had emanated from European clients, resulting in regular deposits of considerable sums within his company's accounts.

The fact that all of these payments came from the same Zurich based bank, had not bothered Albert in the slightest. As is the case with most greedy men, the end tends to cloud the means. His sizeable profits allowed Albert to install electric lighting throughout his new warehouse. This action proved of immense benefit since, it permitted the employment of *shift workers* to attend to the orders of client's requiring a 24 hour dispatch and delivery service, unheard of in other companies.

As his business grew, so did his prestige within the town.

By July, 1901, Albert had been invited to join the board of the local Chamber of Commerce and approached by the local branch of the Liberal party to offer himself for election as town councillor.

In June, 1902, Councillor Smith met, wooed and wed Mary, the youngest daughter of a well-established estate agent and shortly thereafter, moved into a delightful town house in the most sought after section of the town.

By December, 1903, the happy couple had been blessed by the arrival of twin boys who both, having survived the vagaries of childbirth, enjoyed a most robust health.

By the advent of 1906, Albert had become one of the town's most prominent businessmen whose annual European holidays were the talk of the town.

As he stood within the somewhat dusty confines of his warehouse and surveyed the mountains of stacked goods, he should have been the happiest man in the world. But he wasn't Albert Smith and his grocery empire was as false as a flying flat fish.

Born Albrecht Schmidt in Danzig, East Prussia on the 23rd. August 1866, he was only 4 years old when Bismarck created the new unified state of Germany.
Following compulsory military service in the German army, he had decided to make a career in law and applied for a place in the University of Leipzig.
Unknown to Albrecht, his military training had attracted the attention of certain senior officers, both for his effort and success in undertaking the most difficult actions and more to the point, his frequent outbursts amongst his comrades, about the need to show total loyalty to Germany and the Emperor.

Shortly before he was due to take up his place as a student of law, he was visited by the two gentlemen who would alter his future life completely.

The gentlemen stated that they represented an organisation known as the *Aussland Gerichts Dienst des Deutches Reichs* whose sole purpose was the protection of German interests outside the Second Reich.
They informed Albrecht that the time had now arrived where his accepted loyalty might be given a far more positive purpose.
The men explained to Albrecht that, should he seek to perform this service, he would be well-rewarded and

that his future would be one of ease and luxury. The only request was that he leaves his country of birth and moves to England.

He had also been informed that whereas he might never be required to repay the offered benefits, there might arise a moment when, if called upon, he would be required to undertake a reciprocal act that was requested by his country and thus unavoidable.

Albrecht's avaricious urges had been highly stimulated by this information and thus, it took but a further quarter of an hour, before he had become a German agent.

Albrecht's natural linguistic ability accompanied by an intensive training course upon colloquial English, allowed him to slip into England and arrive in his designated town of Portsmouth in early 1892

For many years, he had little contact with the men or their organisation and with his local success within the Portsmouth community, his earlier meeting and commitment began to sink into an uncomfortable memory.

The appearance of the two gentlemen purporting to be members of the German Security Service in late 1906, both shattered his illusions of a continued life of wealth and luxury and brought him down to earth. He had incurred a debt that had to be repaid and he realised that his paymasters would not be easy to ignore, should he fail to fulfill.

Albrecht was informed that his assistance was required in an act, vital to the security of the German state and that he should avail himself and one of his provision carts for a date towards the end of October. The exact time would be made known to him, nearer a finally agreed date.

He was also warned in the plainest terms that he should say nothing of this to anyone -- even his doting wife.

Following this short discussion, the men left.

Whereas the meeting had occurred some five weeks earlier, it was only yesterday that he had received a message to expect the arrival of several men upon the following night.

As Albrecht waited nervously within the vast, illuminated warehouse, he had cause to rue the day that he had so willingly accepted his current status.

Baker Street, London, October 1906

"I believe that it is my game," said Holmes softly. I ignored his comment and regarded the board. Yes! My queen stood proudly and as I believed, controlled the future play. My knight lurked to counter any my move by my adversary. My bishop controlled any diagonal action upon his part, and I had two pawns waiting to booster any move to avoid my assured checkmate.

"My dear chap," I countered, "I have you cornered. You are checkmated in two."

Holmes looked up, grinned and took a large sip from his brandy glass. "Ah! Watson," he mused. "Always the attacker and never considering your defence. Look, if you will upon the board and understand. In relying upon the strength of your queen -- you have failed to observe my remaining bishop and more to the fact, my king's castle. Your queen, upon which you place so much value, is only of any use if she is not taken. I have a move ahead of you which threatens your queen. You have to take my queen for if not, I shall take the only piece that holds your attack together. Once your queen is lost, I have only to move my castle, to force you into an inescapable situation that will ensure my final and irreversible position as your champion."

I looked hard at the board and then, looked again. The man was right! Those little, brown and cream squares that had so recently been my friends -- now glared back at me with a malevolency that shocked my senses. My trusted queen, upon whom I had placed my trust -- now appeared to me, to be more Anne Boleyn upon the day of her execution. I sighed, sat back in my winged chair and reached for my own glass. "I fear that you may be correct, Holmes," I sighed. "I also harbour the conviction that, I shall never better you at this game."

Holmes grinned. "Give yourself time, my dear friend. Who can foresee what may happen?"

I ignored his last comments and noticed that Holmes having replenished our now empty glasses had seated himself within the leather confines of his favourite chair. He waved to me to take the other glass and take the twin chair, facing his own. My slight anger in my

13

current failure to master my good friend subsided as I sipped the fiery liquid and settled myself before the warm glow of the embracing embers of the evening fire.

For a few moments, Holmes contented himself in staring into the flaming grate then, he looked up at me.

"It would seem that our presence is required in Whitehall tomorrow, Watson," he murmured.

"By whom?" I enquired. Holmes handed me a sheet of paper. "See for yourself, my dear friend," he replied. I took the paper and studied the contents.

It was a billet, the kind of communication that gentlemen of our time preferred to adopt to communicate, without the use of the telegraph or postal services. The paper itself had been folded and I opened the message. The writing was bold, perhaps too bold and too brief, for it announced.

"I am instructed by the Foreign Secretary to meet with you and advise you of a serious matter concerning national security. I shall therefore require your most urgent presence at my offices in Whitehall. Failing your reciprocal communication that you are physically unable to meet with this request, I shall expect to meet with you at my offices at eleven o'clock tomorrow."

The note bore the signature in an indescribable hand, beneath which an addendum announced that the writer was a Spencer Ewart who enjoyed the title of Head of Military Intelligence."

"What can he want? I enquired.

"Of that, Watson," replied Holmes, "I have as much

14

idea as you. Still, the paper upon which it is written is of excellent quality, and the request appears to have come from the highest quarters. At the present moment I have little to occupy my active mind. Let's see what occurs tomorrow."

Holmes drained his brandy and sighed. " I'm in the mood for an hour upon my Stradivarius," he announced. This statement was far too much for me. Vanquished after what I considered a brilliant move upon the chess board
-- the prospect of an interminable sixty minutes of Holmes upon his prized "fiddle," was too much to contemplate. Feigning tiredness and excusing myself, I went to bed.

I did not sleep well, being incessantly troubled by what I believed to be a bilious condition which I put down to my consumption of several dozen, Colchester "Pyfleet" oysters at my Wheelers the previous evening.

Thus, I avoided Mrs. Hudson's provision of smoked Lowestoft kippers upon the morning's breakfast table -- contenting both myself and my intestinal confusions, with several slices of toast and several cups of deliciously, dark Assam tea.

Having attempted to receive some little nourishment, I sought the quiet comfort of my fireside chair, thankfully acknowledging the fact that, Mrs. Hudson's earlier efforts within the grate had resulted in the provision of a most comforting inferno. I began to feel better.

Hardly had my earlier troubles attempted to return to

15

normal when Holmes's voice interrupted my comfortable reverie.

"Come Watson! A little haste if you will. We are due at Whitehall at eleven and it is well near ten of the clock and you are not dressed, Stir yourself man!"

Road outside Portsmouth, October, 1906

The man who had initially approached Albrecht within the confines of the warehouse that evening in the company of some ten others was obviously the leader of the rest, and although he had never identified himself, appeared to be in total command. Having selected one of the largest wagons from the collection at the far side of the warehouse, the man ordered Albrecht to harness his horses to the vehicle and drive both he and his companions to the naval dockyard.

Albrecht, his wagon and horses, with the others concealed under a large tarpaulin that completely covered the rear of the conveyance, made their way to the entrance to the dockyard.

Albrecht knew the sentry well.

"Hello, Albert," You're a bit late tonight," said the guard.

"You know me," was all that Albert could say. "When the Navy wants something – it's got to be right away."

The other grunted his assent and moved to raise the bar that prohibited any further access into the harbour confines.

At that precise moment, a shadow appeared behind the sentry and Albrecht caught the glint of a naked blade before it was buried within the neck of the unsuspecting guard.

In his horror of witnessing the deed, Albrecht dimly realised that two other forms had appeared and entered the gatehouse to the dock. Within moments, the three forms had returned to Albrecht's waggon and a voice muttered in his ear, "Drive on!"

In his current mental condition, with his senses reeling, Albrecht had little alternative but to obey.

Arriving beside the massive warship, he was instructed to halt.

Albrecht did as he was instructed. He had little alternative.

In a mental daze, he dimly realised that several other men had emerged from the confines of his wagon and made their ways, quickly and silently to other areas of the dockyard.

Four shadowy forms speedily climbed the long gangplank to the vessel and disappeared within its huge bulk.

Albrecht sat impassively. His brain frozen by the horrors that he had recently evidenced.

Dimly, his addled senses recorded the conveyance of several items from the warship and their loading into the confines of the wagon.

His rapidly departing mental acceptance of ordinary life was rapidly brought back to a sense of normality by the voice.

"Now, get this wagon out of the dockyard as quickly as possible!" commanded Moran

Albrecht did as he was ordered.

Some three miles out of Portsmouth and little having been said by any party, Albrecht's earlier horror of the actions that he had been forced to witness began to turn into a feeling of abject remorse. The wagon was already several miles from Portsmouth. How long was he expected to remain with it? Had he not done enough to satisfy his German masters? Surely, whoever they were must realise that he needed to return to his loving wife. How long did they expect him to remain with them? He had to ask, the question. He spoke to the leader of the men who had been silent since they left Portsmouth.

"Will you require me to drive this wagon much farther?" he enquired nervously. The other appeared preoccupied with his own thoughts, so Albrecht asked again.

Moran looked about him. "No," he muttered. "Pull over to the side of the road. You can go."

"But how do I get back to Portsmouth?" wailed Albrecht.

"That is your problem," stated Moran. "A good walk will do you good. As far as I am concerned, you have served your purpose."

Albrecht failed to appreciate the menace of the other's remark.

Bringing the horses to a halt and handing the slack reins to the other, he turned to get down from the wagon.

He never heard the loud crack of the explosion nor felt the impact of the Mauser's bullet as it entered his skull. By the time his body had tumbled to the roadway, he was dead.

Sebastian Moran replaced the weapon within his

waistband.

Climbing down from the wagon he pulled back the large tarpaulin and spoke to the men crouching within the vehicle.

"Two of you -- put that body in that field!" he commanded, pointing to an area of the roadway to the left of the wagon.

"Won't someone identify him, sir?" said a voice in the darkness.

Moran sighed and stepped down from the wagon.

"Turn him over, face up!" he said.

When this was done, Moran took out his pistol and fired two further rounds into Albrecht's face, obliterating any identifiable features.

"That will suffice," he murmured.

Moran replaced the smoking weapon.

He was about to climb back onto his seat then stopped and dropped back onto the road.

"Bring the lantern here," he ordered.

When this was done, Moran returned to Albrecht's lifeless form and ran the light over the body.

"There is a ring on his right little finger. Remove it!"

One of the men from the back of the wagon tried for several seconds then gave up.

"It won't come off," he announced.

Moran turned to the others. "Any one of you has a knife?" he asked.

One of the men drew a long blade from a sheath, slung from his belt and handed it to Moran who taking the knife, knelt beside the body.

He worked quickly. There was the soft sound of a crunch and one of the other men turned away and retched loudly. Moran stood up clutching the severed hand which he casually tossed into the back of the waggon.

"We cannot afford any form of identification," he announced briefly. "The man's ring might possibly have afforded a clue to his identity whereas his facial features will not."

"Now," he commanded, "we have little time in which to be away from this area and, a long way to travel. We must be off now!"

Whitehall, London, October, 1906

.

The brilliant afternoon sunshine bathed London in an aura of polished magnificence where, to any privileged to observe, none might question its rightful position as capital city of the greatest empire upon the entire Earth.

As our hansom cab, made its way from our lodgings in Baker Street to Whitehall, I had time to consider our present situation.

We were to meet with a, Spencer Ewart -- the recently appointed Director of Military Operations at the War Office.

Both Holmes and I had little idea about the reason for our visit, but as the original request emanated from the Minister of War himself -- we had little option but to accede.

Whitehall positively gleamed with silent authority, its massive buildings perfect in their architectural construction, proclaimed their mighty guardianship of a far-flung empire. As I sat quietly within the cab, my heart was near to bursting, in my pleasure of being an Englishman.

Turning off Whitehall into Horseguards Avenue, our conveyance drew up before a large stone building bearing a brass plate that announced the same to be the Directorate of Military Intelligence. Upon entering the building and our credentials being supervised and accepted by a most officious warrant officer, with an overbearing nature more suited to an "operetta" by Messrs. Gilbert & Sullivan, we were shown up several flights of stairs to that grand, mahogany door, upon which a further brass plate announced the presence of The Director of Military Intelligence, whom I supposed could be expected to be within.

Our officious guide knocked peremptorily upon the door, opened the same and announced in the most stentorial voice, "A Mister Holmes and Doctor Watson to see you sir!" and then ushered us into the room.

Stadschloss, Berlin, February, 1906

"You requested an audience, Herr General," said the Kaiser. "Please proceed?"

Somewhat nervously, Von Schiffert began.

"It has come to the attention of the High Command that the British Royal Navy is currently experimenting with the possibility of a new and dangerous weapon, Your Majesty."

"Ah! You refer to this new battleship," said the Kaiser.

"No, Your Majesty," replied the general. "I refer to an ancillary ordnance that together, with the acknowledged firepower of their latest warship, would render any future naval action against Great Britain as futile as say, a dispute between a tiger and a rabbit."

"Tell me more!" commanded the Kaiser.

Headquarters, Military Intelligence, Whitehall, October, 1906

The figure that rose from behind his desk to welcome us wore the uniform of a lieutenant colonel.

I had expected him to be much older yet the man who took our hands, seemed barely above his middle 30s.

"I have ordered a pot of tea, gentlemen," he began. "I trust that this action meets with your requirements?"

Holmes inclined his head.

"Splendid!" he remarked.

Tea was served and the room left to ourselves. It was Holmes that broke the ensuing silence. "May I enquire why you wish to meet with us," he began.

Spencer Ewart replaced his tea cup and his features became fixed. "You know of "Dreadnaught" he enquired.

"Yes," replied Holmes. "She is said to be the mightiest warship ever constructed."

"Quite so," replied Spencer Ewart. "She is! Her mere presence upon the oceans of the world -- renders any other navy's warships obsolete. She is, in a single stroke, almighty and indestructible to any who might seek to oppose her."

"So what may I enquire is the current upset?" said Holmes. "For I fear that our presence here, must involve some unforeseen naval mishap. Has this behemoth of the seas been stolen?" Spencer Stewart shook his head.

"Not she, Mr. Holmes," he replied. "Yet, 10 men are dead because of something that she carried. Shall I explain?"

Spencer Ewart rose from his chair and crossed to the door, gently opened it, peered outside than closed it and returned to his seat.

"I am instructed by the highest authority to impart to you both information of utmost secrecy to this nation's security," he began. "I am also informed that you Holmes possess an intellect far beyond most others and demand exact detail to the smallest evidential particle, before pursuing your investigations."

"There your information is totally correct, colonel" he replied.

Spencer Ewart lounged back into his chair and sighed deeply. "What does the name Christian Huelsmeyer mean to you, Mr. Holmes?" he began.

Holmes for once in his life appeared somewhat blank.

"I confess," he replied, "that the name means absolutely nothing to me."

Spencer Ewart bent and opened a drawer in his desk, extracted two files and placed them upon his desk. His finger tapped each file and gazed at us both.

"These documents attest that you both enjoy the highest security clearance within the organisation which I represent," he murmured. "It is upon the information contained within these two files, that I am empowered to continue our conversation further." He turned to me. "From the contents of your file, Dr. Watson, I note that you sought fit to refuse the highest award this country might bestow, following your actions in the recent South African war. Might I enquire why?"

I began to feel distinctly uncomfortable.

"I was only doing my duty," I offered. "Nothing more."

Spencer Ewart actually gasped. "My God, Watson! You personally brought back wounded soldiers under intense fire. You were a doctor, not a stretcher-bearer."

"They were away attending to other casualties at the time," said I. "I was the only one available at the time."

Spencer Ewart turned to Holmes. "You are most fortunate, Mr. Holmes, to have as your assistant, a man that is not only brave but modest."

Holmes looked at me and smiled. Then turned back to Spencer Ewart. "Not an assistant but a colleague," he replied. "And a man to whom I would entrust my very life, if need be."

The other took my friend's rebuff without comment. Holmes uncrossed his seated legs and leaned towards the other.

"I believe that you enquired upon our knowledge of a gentleman by name, Huelsmeyer. Perhaps you now feel able to tell us why?"

Spencer looked at the files upon his desk and shrugged.

"It would appear that you are both cleared by my section to be advised upon matters considered to be of the highest security to this government."

Holmes grew impatient. "Come, come sir! You toy with us. That fact has already been established. What is your purpose?"

For a second, Spencer Ewart looked confused. It was plainly obvious that he had never been addressed by any in this fashion before. But the man was intelligent and quickly realised his error.

"Let us discuss wireless transmissions," he stated. Holmes brightened. "You refer to the ability to transmit electrical pulses from one object to another" he remarked."

"Precisely!" agreed Spencer Ewart. He paused (as if considering his next words) then replaced the two files in the drawer from which they had been taken and again looked up at Holmes.

"A few nights ago, His Majesty's dockyard at Portsmouth, within which lies the future pride of the British Navy, suffered an invasion by unknown others which, apart from the ignominy afforded by this incursion into a most protected area, resulted in the deaths, no murders of eight naval ratings standing upon sentry duty and the further deaths of a warrant officer and rating within the port guardhouse."

"Are you telling me that these unidentified villains, whoever they may be, absconded with the ship?" remarked Holmes rhetorically. Spencer Stewart failed to realise his humour.

He returned to another drawer in his desk and extracted a green file. I was able to note that the file was marked "Top Secret" and further, that the top right hand corner of the document had been coloured red.

Spencer Ewart flipped open the file and looked at both of us.

"The ship remains where she has been for several months," he began. "It is the disappearance of an item within the vessel that causes His Majesty's government its present concern. Before I tell you of what we currently know -- I must return to Christian Huelsmeyer.

"Huelsmeyer is a German inventor who has recently applied for and obtained a patent for a machine he has called the Telemobiloscope.

"As you have previously stated, Mr. Holmes, electrical transmissions may be initially transmitted and received by a corresponding receptor -- hence the wireless telegraph. However what is generally unknown, is that such transmitted electrical impulses also have the ability to reflect from any metal objects they encounter and rebound back to the transmitted source. If a reciprocal detector of these rebounded signals might be developed then an accurate position of any metal object would be more than a possibility."

"I begin to understand the point of our meeting," remarked Holmes. "Please continue."

"Christian Huelsmeyer has so far perfected the process

of identifying the position between ships upon the oceans of the world," he continued. But, position only, as far as the compass is concerned. It fails to ascertain the relevant distances between the one from the other. If a similar machine might be developed to calculate that fact then, the possibility of collision, which so often occurs in these days, might be easily avoided. The presence of fog and inclement weather has little effect upon the operation of Huelsmeyer's submitted patent."

Holmes sat bolt upright in his chair and his eyes gleamed with interest.

"My God!" cried Holmes. "The perfection of this machine to which you refer, will be of incalculable value upon aspects of future naval warfare."

Spencer Ewart smiled slightly.

"I can see that you are ahead of me, Holmes," he murmured. "What if I were to tell you that such an instrument has been perfected by our own, Signor. Marconi?"

Holmes appeared fascinated.

"My God!" he breathed. "Such a device might readily be employed to determine the presence of an enemy battle fleet bent upon an attack on this country. Depending upon the range of this device -- an opposing force might easily be dispatched to counter any such menace, before the enemy is within striking distance of their object." He sat back in his chair. "And you say that such a device might exist?"

Spencer Stewart nodded.

"Only within its most basic form at present, yet tests

have shown the same to be most effective and accurate."

"I must congratulate you," replied Holmes. "For you appear to have, if not a future war winner then at least, a naval first that might lead, in the case of our country that relies upon our naval supremacy, to a master card in naval warfare."

Spencer Ewart again shook his head. "You are correct in your assumption, Mr. Holmes," he said sadly.

"Unfortunately, the item of our recent conversation, or rather, an experimental example, had been installed within the vessel of which we originally spoke. I have to tell you that this vital piece of equipment has been found to be missing following the murderous incursion by others into our dock yard."

Holmes said nothing upon this statement, merely fiddled with the pockets of his coat. I noticed this and knew it to be his wish to discover the location of his Meerschaum.

"Your lower left," I advised. Holmes looked at me, nodded and sought within the area upon which I had advised. Then grinned and extracted the pipe. He looked at Spencer Ewart to seek the other's approbation and receiving a salutary gesture, produced a packet of lucifers and lit the thing. For a few moments he puffed and the room suffered the bluish fumes of his exhalations. He spoke to Spencer Ewart.

"Accepting that the theft of the item concerned is not the work of common burglars," he began. "It must therefore be the result of the activities of a foreign power. Do you agree?"

"Entirely so, Mr. Holmes." replied the other. "If this is so, what are your other deductions?"

"We are then left with three, current European powers who envy our naval predominance in the world and see themselves strong enough to oppose, what they consider our empirical projections," replied Holmes.

"And they are?" enquired Spencer Ewart.

"Russia, France and Germany," replied Holmes, without pause. "However France fears the might of a newly emerged Germany upon her borders and now seeks our friendship. I believe that we may omit her from our current equation.

"Quite so," replied Spencer Ewart. "And, the other two?"

"Russia has her own problems," continued Holmes. "Her double defeat by the Japanese navy only last year, has left her battle fleets in a most disastrous situation. The young Tsar has little military knowledge and relies upon the advice of his, highly appointed relatives who in turn, base the same upon historical engagements of the last century.

"I would be more than surprised if Nicholas of Russia had either the will to mount an exercise against this country or the ability."

"That leaves Germany," remarked Spencer Ewart.

"It would appear so," said Holmes, who continued, "Chancellor Bismarck's collation of the various, individual German principalities into a single German state, was accepted by the whole of Europe as a master stroke in diplomacy. Bismarck was regarded as both a social reformer and a man who sought a stable situation throughout the whole of Europe. However, his abrupt dismissal by the new German Kaiser, who seeks nothing but autocratic control of the country that he has inherited -- has caused concern within the neighbouring countries that border his new empire. I fear that any concern upon the future safety of Europe, may reside upon the nationalistic ambitions of the German Kaiser."

"Then our current problem is of German origin?" remarked the other.

"It would certainly appear so," Holmes replied. "I need to complete a few other experiments before I will be able to state categorically the nationality of the perpetrators of this infernal plan."

Spencer Ewart looked up at Holmes and his face brightened. "Can you stop the stolen equipment from reaching those that may use it against us?" he asked and his voice was little more than a whisper.

Holmes inclined his head. "You tell me that the items concerned were stolen from a warship berthed in Portsmouth at the time of the robbery," he began, "I must now enquire as to the weight and portability of the items concerned."

"As to the equipment designed to broadcast the initial, searching signal," replied Spencer Ewart, "the same would occupy the dimensions of a small room. Say, 12 feet by 9. But these measurements are based upon the actual size of the experimental product. It is hoped that with improvements the scale will be dramatically reduced."

Holmes nodded impatiently. "Quite so, quite so, my dear chap. I am little interested in what might be only in current fact. As far as you have told me, somewhere near a cart-load of vital equipment has been stolen from Portsmouth. Am I correct?"

Spencer Ewart nodded.

Holmes continued to press his enquiries. "You refer to broadcasting equipment only," he stated. "Is there more that I should know?" Spencer Ewart appeared somewhat ruffled by being questioned in this matter, yet he controlled his answer in the most diplomatic fashion.

"I fear that there is a further item," he began. Holmes's eyes gleamed.

"Ah! What might that be?"

"The apparatus stolen contained two parts. A projector and a receiver. The latter was necessary to receive signals bounced back from an object encountered by the projector."

"And this too is missing?" enquired Holmes.

Spencer Ewart nodded.

Holmes shook his head depreciatingly.

"From what you tell me, Spencer Ewart, a most highly secret device has been stolen by agents definitely hostile to this country and what is more, in a closely guarded sector and completely under the noses of National Security. Would I be correct in my assumption?"

When Spencer Ewart said nothing, Holmes rose from his chair, placed his right hand upon his hip and paced the room twice before returning to stand before Spencer Ewart's desk.

"I assume that, having failed to deduce who may have perpetrated this larceny, you wish me to assist you and the government in determining exactly who these people may be and assist in the recovery of the stolen items. Am I correct?"

"Precisely!" replied Spencer Ewart. Holmes returned to his chair and caught my eye.

"You may inform the individual who asked you to contact me that both my colleague and I will ensure our best endeavours to bring your current concerns to a successful conclusion," he said.

At that Spencer Ewart relaxed into his chair.

"Thank you, Mr. Holmes. That was all I was hoping for." he sighed. "For, I am given to understand that you well may be the only person able to do so and in so doing, save this country from a most damnable and unworthy fate.

"Come, come, my dear fellow. Do you believe that the theft of a couple of items, you freely admit to be only under development by our scientists at present, really presents a menace, likely to affect the structure of our Empire?"

"Just so," replied the other. "The items to which you

refer have the ability to completely alter the course of naval warfare. A foreign power, capable of refining these objects into their possible end use, will have the ability to control the high seas to an invincibility yet unimagined."

Holmes sat bolt upright in his chair. "If I understand you correctly," he began. "England's acknowledged mastery of the oceans and more importantly, her sea-lanes which are vital to the import of materials, most necessary to her existence might, if this device falls into the hands of a foreign power, render our current position within the world, as ineffective as say, a Pompeian resident with an umbrella upon the day Vesuvius erupted."

Spencer Ewart permitted himself a brief smile. "Your analogy is most accurate, Mr. Holmes," he began. "Unfortunately, it is also most chillingly correct. A hostile power possessing the refined items so recently stolen from us, would possess the most awesome power of invincibility against an opposing fleet."

"I fully understand your worry, sir," replied Holmes. "Yet at present, I am unable to deduce your immediate concern upon the theft of certain items upon which you must be able to produce copies. The manufacture of the same would induce a situation whereby the 'power' employing the thieves, would be left only with a duplicate of that which you had invented and shortly reproduce. *Quid Pro Quo.* Both sides equal. Mastery of the seas left to the most accurate weapons. No real advantage, either side."

33

Spencer Ewart held up his hand. "All and any original drawings and manufactured equipment were of single nature, Mr. Holmes. There are no copies available. It will take years to produce working drawings to enable manufacture of the same items. What has been stolen may take several years to reproduce, and the thieves or their eventual masters have the ability to create this country's researches and findings into a naval, war-winning weapon, that will render obsolete any primacy we believe we may have invented and thus in one, spurious act, obviated our guaranteed naval supremacy." Spencer Ewart relaxed into the confines of his chair and surveyed Holmes.

"Whereas I appreciate your current concern," began Holmes somewhat languidly, "I fail to understand the urgency within your statements. Surely, as far as I am able to deduce, this…er...gadget or gadgets to which you refer, are only valuable to detect an object that is totally invisible to normal, human vision?
"Surely, current battle actions between ships are conducted within sighting distance -- even closer, if we are still to accept the 'broadside' as being the correct position to engage the enemy?"
Spencer Ewart sighed visibly. "There your knowledge is sadly misplaced, Mr. Holmes. Let me attempt to explain" Spencer Ewart then leant across his desk in a conspiratorial manner. "What I am about to impart to you both," he began, "is a matter of the highest national security. I must ask and require you to let what I may now say, remain within the confines of this office. Do I

have this commitment?"

Both Holmes and I readily agreed, which appeared to satisfy Spencer Ewart, for he continued. "Our latest warship from which the items concerned were stolen has been designed and built to render all other warships obsolete. It is fitted with the most powerful armament currently considered practical to ensure domination over any other vessel in the world.

"The 12-inch naval cannon has a range of some 12 miles. An average man with a height of 5-feet-seven-inches standing at sea level can see an object at somewhere just under three miles. If standing within the upper sections of a warship's conning tower, this ability is increased to approximately eight to nine miles, depending upon the man's elevation above the deck. Thus, you will appreciate, human eyesight is far less than the actual range of the ordnance available.

"You may now realise the importance of a machine that not only can see other vessels at greater ranges but, estimate their exact position where they may be and calculate accurately where they may be effectively engaged and destroyed, without corresponding loss or damage to the ship possessing the missing items."

"Naval warfare is not one of the areas upon which I have so far been involved," remarked Holmes. "What exactly do you require of me?"

"Your help, Holmes," replied the other quietly.

"Of that you may be assured," said Holmes. "However, it is imperative that you inform me exactly who may have knowledge of both the existence of the apparatus and more particularly of its whereabouts."

"Again, this is of paramount secrecy," said Spencer Ewart. Holmes inclined his head in acknowledgement.

"But who might they be?" persisted Holmes.

"The Prime Minister, the First Lord of the Admiralty and myself," he stated.

"Ignoring the possibility that three prominent figures in our present administration might be traitors," remarked Holmes," we are left with the fact that the leak in privileged information was from another source."

"Impossible!" cried Spencer. ""None one else knew of it."

"Oh?" said Holmes. "And what of the hundreds of men employed to manufacture this equipment and further, the thousands used in the construction of the new warship. It would take but a careless tongue to ensure that this information made its way directly to a foreign power where it would not require a mastermind to put two and two together."

For a few seconds Spencer Ewart remained silent then he spoke again. "Do you have any thoughts who might be responsible," he enquired.

Holmes reclined in his chair. "It is not of my nature to make deductions or submissions within what is but an initial meeting," he began. "Then again, the facts upon which you have advised me lead me to conclude that this spurious act was committed under the direct instruction and control of a foreign power." Holmes thought for a moment before continuing.

"To release foreign agents into this country without

knowledge of its particular vagaries would be positively destructive to its proposed outcome. There has to be someone in overall command who knows both the railways and road systems to guarantee any chance of success."

"An Englishman!" gasped Spencer Ewart. "Then he is a traitor."

"Possibly," said Holmes. "But who?"

Suddenly he clapped his right hand to his forehead and his next words were almost a hiss.

"My God! No it cannot be! The man is to my certain knowledge incarcerated within one of His Majesty's most secure mental institutions for life."

"To whom do you refer, Holmes?" asked Spencer Ewart anxiously.

"Moran!" exclaimed Holmes. "Sebastion Moran. Possibly one of the most evil individuals still drawing breath within the entire realm."

"Who is this individual?" enquired the other, for I confess that I have never heard of him."

"A cunning and intelligent individual who possesses no humanity or remorse in disposing of any and all who might affect his ultimate ambition of power and wealth," replied Holmes,

"But you said that this man was safely enclosed within one of our prisons?"

"That is so," replied Holmes. "Perhaps I have been too hasty, yet the entire affair as you have described it to me, reeks of his involvement."

Spencer Ewart picked up a desk telephone, waited and

then spoke into the mouthpiece. "Get me anything you may have upon," he paused and looked at Holmes.

"Sebastian Moran," replied my colleague. "Seek also for a Colonel Sebastian Moran, for the man is in a habit of referring to himself as such."

Spencer Ewart imparted this additional information into the mouthpiece then replaced the telephone receiver.

"It may take few moments to discover what intelligence we may have collected concerning this particular individual," he said. "In the intervening moments, perhaps you would be kind enough to inform me, exactly what you personally know about this individual?"

Holmes sat back in his chair and began. "From the information that I have been able to obtain upon the man, I may say with certainty that he was born, the single son, to a somewhat impoverished Suffolk parson in 1856. His early life appears to have attracted little record and his existence becomes officially recorded upon his graduation from military college in, 1875 and his being gazetted a second lieutenant, whereupon he was posted to the Indian sub-continent.

Again, his early regimental life draws little attention, that is apart from his abiding love of the card table and sadly, its accompanying losses which, appear to have been quietly settled by an unknown benefactor in England.

Luckily for Moran, his period of turpitude within the lazy atmosphere of barrack life was cut short by, the troubles that flared upon the northwest frontier.

Sent with his regiment into the Kyber Pass, he was involved in various skirmishes with Afghan insurgents, resulting in the death of his senior officer and a personal dispatch upon his own valorous conduct by his colonel.

Moran's promotion to captain shortly followed. After this event, information upon the notorious colonel becomes somewhat clouded. It is recorded that he led his company upon a near suicidal attack upon the palace of the Sikh Rajah, Suleb Khan, and was shortly thereafter promoted to major but, following this action, little exists upon the man other than the fact that sometime in, 1890, he suddenly left the British army and returned to England where, I had my first opportunity to encounter the fellow."

"So that is all that is known of the man?" enquired Spencer Ewart.

"Apart from the fact, Colonel Sebastian Moran or, whatever he chooses to refer to himself as, is an acknowledged expert in all forms of small arms and moreover, is a deadly marksman with them all," replied Holmes sagely.

"You appear to know of this man well?" said Spencer Ewart. Holmes grimaced. "I have failed to inform you of what became of this individual," he began, "for there is more."

The other said nothing and awaited my colleague's further information.

"Upon his return to this country and for some reason that I am unable to deduce, the wretch both met and fell under the diabolical influence of the most evil man of our century." said Holmes flatly.

"Moriarty?"

"Precisely!"

"But Moriarty is dead," said Spencer Ewart

"Yet, but his spawn lives on," replied Holmes. "He is possibly the only individual capable and willing to organise and carry out the current theft, for I believe for a fact, that he has little affection for his country of birth and for some reason, would welcome an opportunity to provoke any act that might damage the power of Great Britain."

Holmes's comments were halted by the entrance of a young man, dressed in the uniform of a second lieutenant. The arrival placed a green folder upon Spencer Ewart's desk and retired. Spencer Ewart opened the file and studied it for a few moments then closed the document and looked up at Holmes. His face was impassive.

"It appears from our intelligences that a certain prisoner managed by unknown means to escape from His Majesty's Asylum for the Criminally Insane in Broadmoor, some ten months ago," he began. "Believing that the lunatic had left the country and further, wishing to avoid the publicity of the press, upon an escape from what is considered a secure hospital, the Home Office blocked any report upon this occurrence in the public's interest."

Holmes sat straight up in his chair. His eyes flashed.

"The man's name?" he hissed.

Spencer Ewart sank back into his chair and his right hand, flopped lamely upon the closed green file upon his desk. When he replied, his voice was more a consigned whisper. "Moran."

For a second Holmes said nothing, though his facial features tightened visibly. When he spoke again, his voice was low and controlled.

"Then I fear that we are probably up against the devilish and un-restricted actions of one of the most merciless villains in recent history," he said.

"Are you certain that this may be our man?"

"No!" replied Holmes. "Yet the fact that he is abroad and is eminently capable of planning such a deed, makes him my chief suspect.

"Do you possess any further information upon this robbery? Even the smallest detail may prove important?

Spencer Ewart studied the file before him and looked up. "A body was discovered a day ago, some miles from Portsmouth. The man had been shot through the back of the head and dumped in a field. I must confess that I have paid little attention to the unconnected murder of an individual within my current concern upon our country's safety."

Holmes sat bolt upright. "My God! Man, what you have so easily dismissed, might possibly lead us to the crux of this matter. Has a post mortem been carried out?"

The other looked blank. "Not as far as I am aware," he replied

"Then please instruct your most competent pathologist

to attend and examine the body as soon as possible," said Holmes. "Instruct your man to pay the greatest attention to the bullet wound and the diameter of the bullet, found within the dead man's skull. I shall expect the man's full report upon my return from Portsmouth. Are you able to provide this information?"

"Of course, Holmes," said Spencer Ewart.

"You plan to visit Portsmouth?"

"Necessarily so," continued Holmes. "I would like the opportunity to examine the scene of the theft."

Spencer Ewart appeared somewhat deflated by the comment. "My dear Holmes!" he expostulated, " I would assure you that my own people have thoroughly examined the site in detail and discovered nothing that would assist our possible intelligence upon this spurious invasion of Britain's security further."

Holmes would not be put off. "Nevertheless my dear chap, I would seek the opportunity to undertake my own discoveries, should they exist. Should you wish me to undertake this investigation further upon your part, it is vital that I commence from the beginning and ignore anything else. Do you understand my reason?"

Spencer Ewart nodded, "My apologies, Holmes. Of course you may continue upon your own investigations. I will advise the dockyard of your proposed visit and instruct all personnel to render every assistance you may require. When do you believe you will arrive?"

Holmes stood up and beckoned me to do likewise. "Exactly when did the theft of this apparatus occur?" he demanded.

"Two days ago," replied Spencer Ewart. Holmes was

silent for a few moments.

"If we are correct in both our assumptions that the transportation of the stolen articles is by way of a horse drawn conveyance and further, that the intended part of the coast, planned to be utilized for the items embarcation is from a shore situated within our eastern seaboard then, we may have a little more time to prevent this action that may initially have been considered."

Spencer Ewart brightened. "From what you say, Holmes?" he ejaculated, "We still have a more than even chance to retrieve the items?"

Holmes nodded. "If my deductions are correct and I truly believe that they are," he said, "time is not of the essence to the persons who stole your equipment. Secrecy is their aim.

"Transporting the equipment concerned by cart from Portsmouth to an eastern seaboard, wherever it might be and further, travelling by the most undetected route, will enforce the culprits to adopt any available track or lane other than our established road system between the south and the east. In fact, time is on their side. They will know that following the discovery of the theft of the equipment, every available source will be galvanized to thwart the completion of their final intentions. Thus, their controller, whom I believe to be Moran, will have instructed his agents that stealth and not speed is of the essence."

"How long do you perceive we may have?" enquired

43

Spencer Ewart.

Holmes smiled. "How fast does a horse drawn cart travel in one day," he quipped and then became serious again. "I shall require time to evaluate the possible speed of the wagon in relation to the probable distance to a point where embarcation of the stolen items will be practical," said Holmes. "From my preliminary thoughts, I believe that we may have two weeks, perhaps a little longer, before the articles in question may be irretrievably lost."

"How are you able to be so certain?" interrupted Spencer Ewart. Holmes was silent for a moment.

"If the Germans are to blame," he began, "then they will require some place of embarcation situated within our eastern seaboard to enable their easiest passage to a German anchorage. The coast of Suffolk or Norfolk is the closest shore to any German land area, and following my investigations in Portsmouth, I will have more positive evidence from where this might be."

"But, your time limit of a minimum of two weeks?" said Spencer Ewart.

Holmes continued, "Whoever stole the items will have to make a slow and decidedly dangerous passage from Portsmouth to the eastern coast," he began. "They will have accepted that once alerted, our security forces will be searching every accepted highway thus their passage will have to be accomplished upon routes or tracks, generally avoided in usual transport. This will involve a far longer journey. Furthermore, at some junction, they will have to cross the Thames River – while avoiding the metropolis of London -- and make their way to a practically achievable route. This in itself will add copious miles to an actual, legally permissible route. To achieve the secrecy they desire, any travel upon selected highways will have to be within the hours of darkness and at a time when law-abiding citizens are abed. Should they manage to reach a part of the eastern coast and seek the North Sea as their method of conveyance out of this country then, they may have a further delay with tides and prevailing sea conditions." Holmes thought for a second.

"My goodness!" he ejaculated. "Forget my two weeks. I believe that we have a little longer at our disposal." Spencer Ewart's face brightened at this comment. Holmes continued. "However, let us assume that time in our case, is of the essence!" he announced loudly. He took out his Hunter pocket watch, opened its cover, briefly studied the face then snapped it closed. "It is now a little before six in the evening," he said. There is an express leaving Waterloo station to Portsmouth at eight o'clock. Both Watson and I will arrive at the dockyard a little after ten thirty. As, I believe that my investigations at the dockyard may result in my spending a greater amount of time than will allow me to return to London the same day, I would ask you to both seek and make the necessary accommodations for the night? Are you able to effect this small service?"
"It will be as you wish, Holmes," replied Spencer Ewart. He appeared a little concerned.
"Pray tell me, how you know your movements so

precisely?"

Holmes actually smiled. "It is a confounded habit of mine," he began, "to study and retain within my brain, both departure and arrival times of the rail systems of this country. Though tortuous and mentally debilitating to my other mental requirements, I have discovered the same to be most advantageous to situations upon which I have been employed."

"I am more than naturally impressed," gasped Spencer Ewart. "I begin to realise why you are so valued by those with whom I have spoken."

"As any deductions upon my part will be formalised prior to my return to London," stated Holmes, "I shall present myself at your offices no later than ten o'clock upon the day after tomorrow. I noticed that Holmes was about to leave the meeting, yet he paused.

Holmes beckoned me and moved to the door of the room. It was at this point that Spencer Ewart spoke again. "Before you leave, Mr. Holmes, I would offer my best wishes for the success of your coming investigations. What you are about to attempt if unsuccessful, will possibly result in both this country's loss of its mastery of the oceans of the world that guarantees the safety of this island and furthermore irrecoverably tarnish the honour of our nation."

For a few seconds Holmes looked back at Spencer Ewart, then to me. "Come Watson," he announced. "The game's afoot, and we must perforce be gone. Whatever my thoughts, time may still prove to be of the essence."

Without more ado, we left the room.

Stadtschloss, Berlin, March, 1906

"So what of your final plan?" enquired the Kaiser.
"It is perfected, Your Majesty," replied von Schiffert.
"It needs only your agreement for the proposed action
to proceed."
"Am I assured that success or failure of this, shall we
say 'exercise,' will in no way result in any political
embarrassment to your Kaiser?" asked the German
emperor.
"Of that fact you may rest assured, Your Majesty,"
replied von Schiffert. "Nothing can ever be attributable
to your excellence." The Kaiser smiled.
"Good! I shall require you to brief me with the entire
operation from beginning to end," responded the
Kaiser. "If I consider the proposed exercise both
feasible and necessary, then I have nothing further to
say but to wish you luck."

Chapter Two

Waterloo Railway Station, October, 1906

Having seated ourselves within the first-class carriage, we discovered that the only other occupant was a rather elderly gentleman who immediately introduced himself as the Bishop of Mabotoland, excusing his absence from his South African See, due to the onset of haemorrhoids and causing his sudden, yet necessary excursion to the London Hospital in Mile End for the surgical removal of the same. As with most patients, following a hopefully successful surgery, the dear old chap was only too ready to impart what was to him, the mysteries of modern surgery in glorious detail.

Observing that our train had quit the built-up areas of southwest London and accepting that Holmes had little interest in the problems that might beset the extremities of the lower colon and furthermore, the conversion of the inhabitants of South Africa to Christianity where only recently, they had, quite happily, impaled upon huge stakes, any they considered contrary to their beliefs, I suggested that we retire to the restaurant car. Holmes readily agreed to my proposal and I believe that we both inwardly heaved a sigh of relief when, upon my extended invitation to the Bishop, he declined, upon the grounds that his newly healed operation scar permitted him little movement.

The dining car was thankfully poorly attended, which allowed both my friend and I some moments of conversation without being overheard.

The mulligatawny soup was excellent and the perfectly, pan-fried turbot, a most exciting addition to my respect of railway cuisine. Holmes had ordered a Rhenish wine that, upon being served chilled, provided a most delicious addition to our meal. The brandy balloons, swilling with, 1858 Napoleon, complemented what had been a most acceptable repast and, it was with some misgivings that we left the dining car and made our way, somewhat slowly, back to the bishop.

To our surprise and delight, we discovered that the cleric was fast asleep and he remained so, until our eventual arrival at Portsmouth.

Portsmouth Railway Station, October, 1906

Holmes had shown some concern about our transport from the railway station to the dock itself. Should we seek the services of a cab?

However any such misgivings were set to rest upon our leaving the station by the appearance of a most jovial individual clad in the uniform of a chief petty officer who greeted us with the ripost, "Gentlemen! You must be Mister Holmes and Doctor Watson."

Holmes paused in his passage. "And how may you know that fact, my dear fellow?"

The other smiled broadly. "One such gentleman attired as you, sir with cape and cap and clutching that meerschaum pipe in your right hand as you do sir, can be no other." The chief petty officer turned to me. "And you sir, are surely Doctor Watson, whose stories within the pages of the *Strand Magazine*, so perfectly describe the both of you that, identification upon your presence here is simple."

Holmes smiled. "My God man!" he ejaculated warmly, "you are wasted in your service within our navy. With your intelligence, you might make a great detective." The other grinned broadly at this appraisal.

"Permit me to introduce myself gentlemen," he began. "Chief Petty Officer Davis at your service. Rooms have been reserved for you both at a nearby hotel and a carriage awaits to transport you to your accommodation. Any further service that I may be to you, is yours to command. In short, I am at your complete disposal until your visit is accomplished."

Holmes nodded in appreciation of this service. With that, Chief Petty Officer Davis saluted smartly and showed us to a nearby carriage.

Our conveyance deposited us a nearby hotel and for the life of me, I am unable to recall the name of the hostelry yet, I recall that the meal that we ate as particularly most appetizing.

Holmes ordered, mutton broth, followed by veal cutlets and vegetables "en saison". He was pleasantly surprised to discover several bottles of, Chateau Latour 1904 within the hotel's cellar and, after the first bottle informed me that the same possessed a ready propensity for laying down for, to his acute palate, the wine would possibly become a most sought after fermentation in later years.

Following the consumption of at least a half a bottle of Napoleon, 1898, we happily retired to our separate bedrooms for the night.

We met again the following morning at 8 o'clock and after a breakfast of Scottish kippers, which we were reliably informed by the hotel chef, were daily delivered by express train from the fisheries of Aberdeen, we were told by no less a personage than the hotel manager himself that, a chief petty officer and a carriage outside, awaited our presence.

As usual, I carried the small leather bag that all doctors used but within which, upon this occasion, Holmes had insisted that I use to contain the instruments he insisted were necessary for his investigations.

Davis greeted us and we drove off to the dockyard.

Holmes was his usual self and the sunlit journey from our hotel to the gates of the dockyard through the narrow lanes of the town was most affable.

At one point, Davis remarked, "You may find that Lieutenant Weston's manner is somewhat abrupt, gentlemen. He is young for the position that he occupies and shall we say little schooled in the correct conversation to be employed to others outside the naval service."

Holmes looked at Davis and actually winked his eye. "I believe that we can give as good as we receive, chief petty officer," he murmured. Upon this remark, Davis smiled silently, and no more was said by any of us until we reached the gates of the dockyard where, after a brief conversation between Davis and the sentry, we were ushered into the massive complex. Our carriage eventually drawing up at a small building upon which, affixed to the wall was a polished brass sign bearing the annotation, "Naval Intelligence."

We were met by a junior rating who asked us to follow him inside the building, whereupon we were led to a door upon which bore the sign, Lieutenant Peter Weston. The junior rating knocked at the door and a voice within, bid us come. We did as requested.

Lieutenant Peter Weston, clutching a small wooden board upon which was pinned a sheet of white paper, regarded both Holmes and I with what may only be described as a sense of misgiving.

"You are Holmes and Watson?" were his first words and his manner to my mind was both churlish and arrogant.

"No!" stated Holmes.

At this, Weston completely lost his earlier arrogance and became in an instant, sorely confused.

"Then who the devil are you?" he blustered.

Holmes smiled acidly. "I am, Mister Holmes," he said slowly and turning to me continued. "And this gentleman and, he stressed my title, "is Doctor Watson!"

All at once, Weston became a most pleasant fellow.

"Gentlemen!" he practically honeyed, "Please forgive my initial impudence. Sadly, I am used only to speaking with men who have little regard for politeness and civility. Holmes's attitude relaxed.

"Then perhaps you will permit us a chair, Lieutenant?" he enquired. Weston appeared overly keen to comply and having taken our seats, we awaited Weston's further comments.

"As I see it, Mr. Holmes," he began. "I am to allow you complete control upon your investigations into the current theft of certain items of His Majesty's equipment within this dockyard. Holmes nodded but said nothing.

"I have to tell you, Mr. Holmes," continued Weston, "that my own team has carried out a thorough and complete survey of the scene and has found nothing to indicate exactly who the perpetrators were."

Holmes practically exploded in anger. "What?" he bellowed. You mean to tell me that a crowd of clodhopping ratings has been permitted to blunder through the scene of criminal investigation? My God! Do you consider the damage that their actions may have caused?"

"My men are trained in matters of naval security," bleated Weston somewhat lamely.

But Holmes was in no mood to offer any quarter. "Security?" he hissed. "With respect, sir, I would suggest that any recent investigations upon the part of your staff, may be not only of little value but more importantly, have destroyed vital evidence that I alone might decipher."

Holmes's last outburst was too much for Lieutenant Weston. He rose to his feet. "I must protest your comments sir," he blustered. "My men are fully cognisant with the process of detection in all matters. Your allegations upon our valuable service are most misplaced."

At this, Holmes lost his recent aggression. "I meant no offence, Lieutenant Weston," he crowed in words that leaked honey. "You will appreciate that my work is most usually undertaken upon a crime scene where little has occurred to disturb even the most trivial evidence. Where there have been strangers upon the scene, perhaps not trained within my ways of detection, their actions though unmeant, may destroy even the most flimsiest of clues." Weston relaxed in his chair. "I fear that we may have started off upon the wrong foot, Mr. Holmes," he announced quietly.

At this Holmes brightened considerably. "Then, if that be so, Lieutenant," he began, " I suggest that we discover our right foot and put the same forward."

Without waiting for a reply, Holmes stood up, beckoned me to do likewise and fixed the deflated naval officer with one of his piercing stares. "Come sir!" he announced. "Pray take me to this ship!"

German Military Headquarters, Zossen, Berlin - February 1906

Moran sat alone upon the single chair that faced the large, leather topped mahogany table behind which stood another chair. A huge map of Europe covered most of the existing back wall.

A fire blazed within the grate but did little to expel the unusual presence of cold chill that permeated his backbone.

He had moments in which to assess his current position.

Germany or rather the German High Command had been good to him since his earlier escape from England. He had been provided with more than comfortable lodgings within a most sought after residential section of the German capital. His merest wish had been both accepted and provided without complaint and, a sum, commensurate with that received by a colonel in the German army, regularly deposited within his account at the Deutsche Bank. Life within Germany had been good but it was now time to repay his master's beneficence. What might they seek to demand?

His deliberations were suddenly cut short by the entrance of von Schiffert.

"I trust that you are well and enjoying our hospitality?" murmured von Schiffert conversationally.

"Yes, General," replied Moran. "I find that German life is to my liking."

"Good," replied von Schiffert. "Referring to our earlier

conversation a week or so ago, I must tell you that the time for you to perform a small service for Germany has arrived."

The cold chill within Moran's backbone became an icy floe.

"The Kaiser is most concerned about the recently constructed British battleship known as the Dreadnaught," he began.
"Why this concern?" enquired Moran. "I understand that the Kaiser has ordered the construction of warships of similar or greater propensity to that of the British."
Von Schiffert inclined his head indulgently at this interruption, but continued.

"More to the point, the Emperor's interest is concentrated upon what he has been given to understand, has been placed within her structure."
Moran's own interest was aroused.
Von Schiffert spoke again. "The detection and accurate position of any enemy vessel out of normal visionary parameters, has for many years, avoided the proficiency of naval gunnery so necessary for the conclusion of any long range sea battle. From the information that we possess, we are forced to accept that the British claim to have perfected a device that negates this problem. In short, the Kaiser wishes that we obtain this device, so that the services of the same, if proven to be as accurate as the British believe, will complement German ship construction and achieve parity with Great Britain."

Suddenly, Moran realised what was going to be required of him.

"As I understand this conversation, Herr General, you wish me to formulate a plan whereby this British device may be obtained and transported to Germany?"
Von Schiffert slowly shook his head. "Not just plan. Your physical participation within any such exercise is considered paramount to its eventual success."
Suddenly Moran understood the cold feeling. His senses never let him down.

"If I am to achieve what both you and the Kaiser wish, I shall require a limited period in which to formulate this plan," murmured Moran cautiously.
"Of course!" replied von Schiffert. "Shall we say two weeks?"
Moran nodded. "I shall also require some assistance from others in this matter."
"As the entire operation enjoys the Kaiser's wish, the entire services of the German nation are at your disposal, Colonel," replied von Schiffert. "What do you require?"

Attuned to quick thinking Moran took little time to deliver his initial reply. "I shall require to form a team of say 10 individuals who are both ruthless and able to obey my commands and instructions to the letter without qualms. I am sure that your Secret Service will be able to supply me with such men?"
"That will not be a problem," said von Schiffert.

Moran had not finished. "Furthermore, these men should be of a mental calibre, insofar as they would if necessary cut a stranger's throat for the price of a bag of German marks. When you are seeking to provide these men, I suggest your security services seek the recruitment of dissidents, anarchists and generally known disaffected individuals from neighbouring countries."

"Why so?" enquired the General.

Moran continued. "In the event that any of the selected men are captured by the British authorities, their discovered nationality will never cast any suspicion upon Germany. Then again," he continued," each man should possess a grasp of the English language and able to understand any orders that I might give."

Von Schiffert appeared impressed. "Mein Gott! Moran, I have misjudged you." he breathed.

Moran continued, "The selected team must undergo a period of extensive training under my personal instruction. To maintain the absolute secrecy required by this operation, they must never know my real name. Nor must they have any indication of the identity of the country that is employing them. Only if this is both possible and effected, will Germany's involvement remain a matter of conjecture and not fact."

"But how do you believe that we may recruit and train these men in Germany without them knowing?" asked von Schiffert.

Moran smiled. "That aspect is entirely up to you General. If it were my concern, I would have the men transported within closed and windowless railway compartments to a secure area within Germany's least populated regions. A camp, including an unobserved training area should be made available and the entire complex surrounded by barbed wire fencing and guard posts. Every sentry must be required and able to speak in English only at all times, and the weapons issued to the selected team should be of general European manufacture.

"The men themselves will not learn of the object of their training until the moment that I brief them, shortly before we leave for England."

"But you will speak in English?" questioned the other. "Might that not provide evidence of identity? The British must by now know that you are in Germany and furthermore, your hatred of the country of birth. Even the stupid English can put two and two together and arrive at the figure four?"

The former icy feeling had left his body. Moran realised his purpose and relished in his new sense of power. "Rest assured Herr General," he stated. "Whether the projected operation results in success or failure, it is not my intention that any of my team survive to return to Germany."

Naval Dockyard - Portsmouth, October, 1906

I was astounded at the pure size of the beast that dwarfed the berth in which she lay

She had been designed to destroy any other craft which she might encounter and her huge guns that poked their ugly snouts from massive turrets upon her decks, left few in ignorance of her ability so to do. So confidant of her awesome power had been her designers that they had purposefully omitted weapons of lesser calibre normally installed to combat smaller vessels, leaving them to similarly sized ships of the fleet to dispose of. Her only other offensive armament had been the provision of small caliber, quick firing guns whose purpose was the destruction of any enemy submarines, foolish enough to surface and attack her. Our proscribed attendant, a rather dashing naval lieutenant who introduced himself as Broughton, led us through the main deck and into the base of the towering superstructure in which the robbery had occurred.

The room, or more correctly the cabin, at which we eventually arrived was of the size and dimensions of a family lounge, yet void of any furnishing artefact apart from the ends of cleanly severed electrical cables that hung snakelike from its walls. Broughton who accompanied us, being some 20 years of age appeared most courteous and correct and I, for reasons of my own, yearned to enquire upon his antecedents further. Finally we reached the area in which the robbery had occurred.

The blackish eyes of unbolted holes yawned from the empty deck planks from which the stolen equipment had been removed. The entire floor had been painted with a white covering upon which appeared the imprint of many footsteps.

Holmes cautioned me to tread no further than the bulkhead at which we stood. For moments he surveyed the empty area before us. His eyes gleamed with satisfaction.

"We may be in luck, Watson," he murmured. "The fellow who painted that floor may have unknowingly provided us with a great favour."

"I am sorry," I replied. "But for the life of me, I know not of what you now speak." Holmes winked mischievously.

"The white floor is a perfect reflector of the morning light that now permeates this otherwise dark compartment through the various portholes upon its walls," he began. "The same portholes, due to their acute angle within the ship's sides, also restrict any ingress by the direct beams of the morning sun. The entire scenario is perfect for the investigations that I now will effect."

I looked at Broughton and he at me and it was obvious that neither of us had any clue as to what Holmes referred.

Holmes then took off his shoes: an action totally foreign to any that I had ever seen before within our many investigations. He turned to me, "Now Watson, if you would be so kind, hand me my case."

I did as he bade.

Clutching the case, Holmes made his way gingerly across the floor of the compartment, staring intently at the white floor. Suddenly he stopped, knelt down, opened his case, extracted both his magnifying glass and several white envelopes which he placed upon the floor. He rummaged again within the confines of the leather bag and produced a small brush and equally tiny dustpan which would have warranted more use to a child than an adult.

Very carefully, he stroked the floor with his brush and scooped the contents of the area into the dustpan and from there into one of the white envelopes.

For several minutes this procedure continued, until finally the entire area of the cabin had been covered. Holmes stood up and replaced the brush and dustpan back within his case. He turned to the bulkhead where we stood and addressed Broughton.

"I noticed the presence of many sailors when we came aboard earlier," he began, "may I assume that the ship now has a full complement?"

"You may sir," replied Broughton. "After the incident and with her sea trials imminent, all leave has been cancelled and the entire crew recalled." He appeared nervous when he next spoke. "That is," and his voice had dropped to a most conspiratorial level "apart from a few of the senior officers, who appear to be, currently engaged upon other business, if you get my meaning."

"Then," said Holmes, "the service that I require should be of little problem to a man of your position and ability".

"Name it sir and it shall be done," stated the other

confidently.

Holmes leant towards the man and inclined his head. "I require the provision of a pot of tea and perhaps a few cakes," he stated. "If you are able to provide the same, please include in your request the addition of three cups, so that we may all enjoy a little refreshment at this time."

"I can try, Mr. Holmes," replied Broughton. "But, I am only a junior officer. The first officer, who must by all accounts be upon the bridge at this moment, may have a different idea upon what services I may request and which he is willing to supply."

"Good God man!" exploded Holmes, "Having been required to investigate a crime that may affect the entire security of this country -- am I to be denied a small request for sustenance that will allow me to complete my work?"

Broughton appeared taken aback by this outburst and said nothing.

Holmes continued. "I shall require a period of at least an half an hour in which to finalise my current searches," he said, removing a large tin box which I knew to contain carburundum powder and a fan tailed brush of pure squirrel hair. "More than enough time," he continued, "for you to effect the small service that I require."

As he noticed that both Broughton and I remained stationary at the bulkhead, he added, "Well, be off with you Lieutenant and take Doctor Watson with you. By the way," he added, "You may inform whoever you encounter upon the bridge and whatever his rank that, should he refuse to grant my simple request, his name and rank will immediately be conveyed to the Admiralty. Now, off you go."

We left Holmes and made our way to the bridge. The journey was brief but, it allowed me the opportunity that I sought, to question our guide further.

"Tell me, Broughton?" I enquired. "You name is familiar. Do you have a relative who served in India some 20 years ago?"

Broughton stopped his upward passage and turned to me. "My father, James Broughton commanded the 14th Punjab Horse during that period," he answered.

"Is you father still alive?" I enquired.

Broughton nodded. "My father has but recently retired from the Army," said he. "Both my father and mother have acquired a delightful cottage in Gloucestershire in which to spend their remaining days together."

"Then when you next visit your father," I instructed "make sure that you convey my sincere best wishes for, I served for a short time as medical officer within his regiment."

Broughton appeared pleased at this association and promised to do so. He was about to return to the stairs and I was unable to let the moment pass.

"Please also mention another matter that I and he will share until our dying day. But never within earshot of your dear mother." Broughton was obviously perplexed. I continued.

"The night of the Rajah's Ball,"

"May I learn to what this curious message portends?"

he asked. I shook my head and winked at him.

"It is a private matter between gentlemen," I answered.

"That is enough for you at your age."

With that, we completed our climb to the bridge of the warship.

Broughton's concerns upon the first officer's reaction to Holmes's request for nourishment were unfounded. The first officer, upon learning of my identity, proved to be an avid follower of my previous stories within the pages of the London journal that published the same and far more than acquiescing to Holmes's wishes, insisted we all take our refreshment with him, within the confines of the ship's wardroom.

Afternoon tea was served and Holmes, having cleaned the detritus of the carburundum powder from his hands if not his coat and shirt sleeves, joined us.

Holmes appeared overly excited and our genial conversation within the wardroom was thus brief and truncated. I was mildly interested in a final question that Holmes put to Broughton before we took our leave.

"What is the normal footwear used by your men when investigating a situation such as this?" he enquired.

Broughton appeared quite nonplussed but replied.

"Standard, leather soled shoes, as specified by naval regulations, Mr. Holmes."

Yet Holmes continued, "Do they ever wear rubber footwear, as employed upon a wet deck?"

Broughton thought for a moment then shook his head vehemently.

"Never!" he asserted. "Unless their investigations

concern a sea operation."

Holmes appeared more than satisfied with this answer and having thanked both Broughton and the first officer for their assistance, insisted that we make our way to the railway station, where we were lucky enough to obtain first-class reservations upon the evening London express.

As we settled ourselves within our compartment, I noticed that Holmes appeared to have lost none of the intense excitement that he had evidenced so previously.

"Tell me Holmes," I began, "what have you discovered that makes you so?"

Holmes glowered at me. "You must wait until I have completed my final researches tonight, after we have regained the assistance of my equipment in our rooms," he replied.

"Then if we are to await your further investigations until we reach London, perhaps we may both enjoy the benefits of the catering available within this train," I replied. "I, for one, am starving."

Holmes looked at me and grinned. "Dear Watson," he mumbled in a most friendly manner." I have clean forgot your interminable craving for the consumption of food which bothers me but little, when I am concerned upon a case."

He arose from his seat. "Come, let us eat."

We made our way to the dining car and having been warned by Holmes that our journey would be little more than an hour, restricted ourselves to a somewhat lighter menu than normal.

Onion soup, followed by a delicious segment of steak

and kidney pudding, provided the answer to my current exasperation. Holmes had selected Chateau La Fitte 1903, to compliment or meal. The nose of the wine was delicious, yet I pondered upon the slick, greasy tendrils of glycerine that sloughed their downward way within my glass as evidence as to the wine's alcoholic intensity, as being pertinent to the eventual mental condition required of me upon our eventual arrival at Baker Street. My forebodings proved incorrect for by the time we arrived at Waterloo Station, I was both ready and willing to adhere to any reasonable request made by my colleague.

It was thus, nearer seven o'clock, when our hansom carriage drew up in Baker Street.

Holmes's previous anxiety appeared to have returned in a most elevated state. Upon reaching our rooms, he began organising the various chemical apparatus that always reposed upon the large table in the corner of our main reception salon.

Of interest, I enquired the reason for his haste and he in turn replied, *"Tempus fugit!* Watson. *"Tempus fugit!* my dear fellow, so I declined to seek further.

Holmes turned to me. "Be so kind as to fetch me two volumes that presently repose upon the upper third shelf of my bookcase if you please, Watson." I awaited his further instructions.

"The first volume is titled *Geology and the Suffolk Coast* and the other, *Smuggling in East Anglia.*"

I discovered the tomes without much trouble and returned to Holmes who seemed to have completed setting up the equipment, he believed necessary for his further researches. Rubber tubes stretched from glass beakers into others while the hot, gas driven flame of a bunsen burner, flickered beneath one.

I handed Holmes the volumes that he sought.

"Thank you Watson," said Holmes, to my mind, rather absentmindedly.

"Now, if you will oblige yourself of a pencil and a sheet of paper, I would like you to open and digest the book and note areas of smuggling activities in East Anglia during the latter half of the last century and more, the first half of this one. While you are engaged upon this exercise, I will concern myself with the composition of coastal soils, to which the result of my current experiments and the information supplied within the other book, may point to the spot where these criminals both arrived in the country and from where the intend to leave."

I was astounded by this statement. "How can you possibly deduce this fact?" I enquired.

Holmes offered me a most conspiratorial grin. "You may recall that I asked, Broughton what his men normally wore upon active duty and he replied, leather soled shoes."

I was about to interrupt but he waved me to silence and continued.

"Leather soled shoes leave little evidence upon a floor yet, rubber soled boots, contain tangs or raised ribs upon their soles that produce stability in wet conditions. Unfortunately, these tangs also collect detritus from the soil upon which they have been worn. Small deposits of this always remain within the deeper confines of the sole and may deposit this detritus when dried, within any area in which the boot is then worn."

He beamed wickedly. "I discovered actual samples of this evidence upon my investigation earlier today and from the chemical experiments that I now intend to conduct, hopefully combined with the results of the investigations that I have now required you to complete, it should be possible for me to define within a couple of miles, the point on our coast where these vile criminals landed.

For the next hours, I pored over the recorded information of smuggling activities within the southeastern coastline and made copious notes upon my findings. During this period, I had occasion to look at Holmes and found the same, busily engaged in a variety of movements.

Glass jars were filled with liquids of the most incandescent hues, samples of I know not what, were deposited within bowls of various small plates that littered the top of the large table. From time to time, my colleague peered into the brass microscope that sat at the end of the table and grunted to himself.

Although, I had completed the analysis of my subject matter by ten o'clock, I was obliged to wait a further half an hour before Holmes stood back from his work table, placed his hands upon his hips and turned to me.

"Have you completed your findings, Watson?" he enquired. "For I believe that I have completed mine."

I nodded.

"Good!" exclaimed Holmes. "Then before we compare our joint discoveries and more to the point, allow me to explain to you exactly why it is important that both our works concur, I suggest that we avail ourselves of a glass of Dow's 1898. Would you agree?" I would and did.

Thus, seated within the confines of our leather winged chairs and sipping the elixir of a most sought after port wine, Holmes began.

"The samples that I managed to obtain within the cabin in which the robbery occurred, indicate positively the area of coastline used by the robbers." I obviously appeared nonplussed for he continued.

"Let me attempt to explain. Examination of my samples indicates a basic level of chalk that has been, over the years, covered by a deposit known as London clay. The process to which I refer occurred some 50 to 75 million years ago and evidence of this activity may be seen throughout the coastal regions of East Anglia from the Thames estuary to the northernmost beaches of Norfolk. It is not this mixture that attracts my interest. More to the point, it is the presence of another component that directs me to believe that the area, in which we should now confine our further investigations, may be the actual place of ingress and planned egress of the villains responsible for this abominable crime."

"Then my own researches of the last few hours may be of little use," I began.

Holmes shook his head impatiently.

"All in good time, my dear fellow. Please allow me to continue?" I kept silent.

"Certain areas of this coast contain an additional

material prevalent to only certain stretches of beach," he stated. "This, rather creamy limestone deposit is known as Coraline Crag and I discovered presence of this substance within the samples that I have just analysed. I thus know approximately where these foreign agents may have entered this country and this information, together with your own researches into possible points of entry used by smugglers, should result in my being able to establish the exact position that they seek to use for their embarcation." He paused and sought about himself. "Watson! I require a map of the East Anglian coast. Please be good enough to seek within my map drawer in my bedroom for the same."

As usual, I did as I was bade. However upon my return to Holmes, I was horrified to see that he had cleared our dining table and placed upon the vacant space his small box of water colours together with a water filled, cut glass balloon from a set of six that had been presented to me by the regiment upon my leaving India.

"Holmes!" I protested. "That balloon is one of a set. Its sentimental value to me is beyond price."

""For goodness sake Watson, it is but only a glass. Rest assured that upon completing the action that I am about to commence, it will be restored to you in the pristine condition that it is now." I gave up lamely.

"Now!" said Holmes," you have the map?"

I handed over the rolled paper and Holmes spread the same out upon the table. "Place the two candelabra upon each corner of the top edges, if you will my dear chap," he instructed, "and pass me the two books that rest upon the arm of my chair. They will suffice to secure the bottom corners of the map." This was done and Holmes opened the lid of his paint box, produced a brush and began to mix a colour within the internal segmented sections of the lid. I watched fascinated.

Having completed his mixture of hues, Holmes dipped his brush within the concoction and drew a wet, pinkish line upon the map. It began somewhere close to Great Yarmouth and ended just south of the town of Aldeburgh.

He then continued the line from Southwold and ended the same with a flourish at the mouth of the Thames estuary.

Apparently satisfied with his efforts, he mixed a further colour within his palette and painted a rather bluish slash between the two points. He stood back satisfied.

"There, you see, Watson," he stated triumphantly. "There is where it happened!"

I peered at his efforts. Within the confines of the bluish paint line, the Suffolk coast appeared rather void of population, apart that was, from a small hamlet by the name of Thorpe. Holmes interrupted my thoughts.

"I have further evidence that leads me to believe that my current beliefs are correct," he continued," and before you interrupt my thoughts, as you are continually wont to do, I must tell you that I possess additional information that I feel confirms my deductions."

"Do you wish to see the results of my efforts upon the areas of smuggling?" I attempted vainly.

Holmes shook his head. "Later, Watson," was all he muttered. Then noticing my dismay at his verbal rebuttal, he said softly, "They will be of great use in good time."

I remained silent and awaited his further discourse. I had not long to wait.

"If we, for the present, accept that Germany is the originator and arbiter of this foul deed against a country to which she claims friendship," began Holmes, "then who better to plan and effect this spurious action than an Englishman with naught but hatred for his own kin and who craves the indulgencies that money may purchase without thought for the hurt and damage that his greed may incur. Sebastian Moran is an individual without scruples of any nature and, if persuaded by German gold to turn traitor, would give his *volt face* little consideration."

I felt that I had to intercede. "But why are your thoughts fixed upon this individual and not upon others who may be actively dissatisfied with England and its empirical rule within the world?" I hesitated to enquire as Holmes appeared most positive.

"Several years ago," he replied "when I had established that Moran was set upon my own destruction, I took the trouble to investigate the man's antecedents. I discovered that Moran had been the single progeny of, the Reverend Augustus William Moran who, for a time had obtained a living as the vicar of the joint parishes of Aldringham and Thorpe. I paid scant attention to this information at the time yet now I believe it to be vital to the present matter. Sebastian, his only son, grew up within the area we now believe to contain the coastline within our investigations. As a youth and experiencing as all boys do the spirit of explorations and adventure, he must remember every detail of the area in question, its guarded and free parts, its beaches and safe areas and further, its ancient shacks and sheds ignored by most, where artefacts may be stored without notice for a limited period. That," he concluded, "is why I initially considered Moran to be the prime architect within this hateful conspiracy."

"But the German Kaiser would now consider such an action of war upon his part," I countered.

"He has no need to be involved within any actions that may occur or for that matter result," replied Holmes. "The German Kaiser, though militarily strong upon the land mass of Europe, is far too weak to encroach upon the seaways of the World. He requires a strong battle fleet which at the present time, he does not possess. He envies the power of the British Grand Fleet. Should he gain possession of the stolen articles, their inclusion into his current plans for a comparative naval fleet to counter that of our own, may well prove disastrous in any future offensive action against the Royal Navy."

I couldn't stop myself, and I yawned.

Holmes noticed. "Dear Watson," he said softly, "I forget my interminable misuse of your waking hours. Off to bed with you, this moment!"

I was eternally grateful for his compassion. "Come on Holmes," I began, "You must be exhausted yourself. Let's make a night of it?"

Holmes smiled. "Permit me to calculate the distance and time involved from Portsmouth to the Suffolk coast for our meeting with Spencer Ewart tomorrow whereupon, I will certainly take your good advice my dear fellow," he stated.

Upon that, I retired to my bed.

Stadtschloss Palace, Berlin, March 1906

The Kaiser's cold grey eyes stared unflinchingly into von Schiffert's

"So it has begun," he said simply.

The two men sat in a lavishly furnished ante room within the Emperor's magnificent Berlin palace following an Imperial summons to the meeting.

"Yes, Your Majesty," answered von Schiffert. "Our planning has now reached a stage where, the exact details of the entire operation may be placed before your Imperial Majesty."

"When will the operation take place?"

"Possibly late October, Your Majesty," replied von Schiffert. "My sources inform me that installation of the equipment we seek will not be completed until earlier that month, and as the proposed sea trials are scheduled to commence in early November, prior to the vessel's commissioning into the British Grand Fleet, we have selected the date as being the optimum time for the operation to be carried out."

"And the details of this plan?" enquired the Kaiser.

"The plan involves landing a carefully selected team upon the Suffolk coast of East Anglia, who will make their way to Portsmouth," he began. "Upon reaching the British naval dockyard they will carry out the necessary actions to remove the equipment we desire and thereafter, transfer the same back to the point where they landed. The initial operation is most straightforward and the danger lays within the time that it will take to accomplish the transfer of the stolen articles to Suffolk."

"Why so?" enquired the Kaiser.

"The items that we seek contain a degree of weight unsupportable within a normal carriage," continued von Schiffert. "We are forced to utilise the services of a heavy cart. This in itself presents our first problem."

The Kaiser said nothing and von Schiffert continued. "Accepting that the average speed of a cart upon a normal highway is between 5 to 10 miles an hour and more to the fact that our team will be forced to travel by night to escape detection by the British security services that will have been alerted within hours of the discovery of our theft, further, that any attempt to cross the Thames river by normal crossing will most certainly result in our apprehension, we shall be forced to circumnavigate the British capital by a westerly then northeastern route. This avoiding action will add days to our eventual time of arrival at our designated point of embarcation."

The Kaiser stroked the carefully waxed points of his moustache with his right hand.

"Good!" he murmured softy. Then his eyes hardened. "Are you certain that no blame either actual or inferred, can be attached to Germany and more importantly me?" Von Schiffert was quick to reassure his Kaiser.

"Absolutely, your Majesty. Every possible connection to you or your government, has been scrupulously omitted from the action, whether it succeeds of fails."

The Kaiser's eyes showed little emotion yet his next words betrayed a veiled threat. "You speak of failure, Herr General? Surely, this is not an option?"

A shiver of pure fear ran through von Schiffert's frame. He had said too much. The Kaiser's mood swings were well known to the German court. A moment of gratuitous praise and outlandish flattery for an act of service he found most helpful might be changed into violent diatribe against anyone, whose actions he found unconscionable.

"Your Majesty," he began, "there is in any plan, an element of failure."

"So how long will this journey take?" enquired the Kaiser irritably.

"At least two weeks, maybe more," answered von Schiffert.

The Kaiser rose from his chair. "Keep me informed!" he commanded.

Headquarters Military Intelligence, Whitehall, October, 1906

The morn dawned bright if somewhat chilly. The October sunlight possessed a brilliance that tainted the tumbling leaves of autumn with an intensity so sought and beloved by the artists of our time. The streets gleamed with unwarranted cleanliness and the incumbent air, throbbed with the unheard hum of vibrant life.

For a brief period of time and through the window of our conveyance, I allowed my simple mind to dwell upon the peace and happiness, so evidenced upon the faces of the passersby that reflected my own senses within the country that I so sorely loved. Then reality forced my mind back to the present situation.

Our cab drew up before the building that housed the offices of Military Intelligence and shortly thereafter, we found ourselves seated before Spencer Ewart.

Holmes began to explain the results of our recent visit to Portsmouth.

"In my investigations within the room within which the theft occurred," he began, "I discovered the impressions of several boots, that had not been disturbed by others seeking earlier information upon the robbery. I was able to sketch my findings. I also discovered a collectible detritus of soil left by these items, which I have now analysed.

"I must therefore assume that the perpetrators of this disgusting act, employed the use of this footwear upon their arrival in England and without thinking of cleaning the soles of the same, packed them away for use in the commission of the spurious act of which we now know." Spencer Ewart was unable to contain himself.

"So, what have you found, Holmes?"

Holmes waved the other to await his next words.

"The content of the soil is peculiar to a small part of the east coast between Lowestoft and the small town of Aldeburgh," he continued. "It is there that I believe the original landing and proposed embarcation will occur."

Spencer Ewart was obviously impressed. "My God! Holmes, you've cracked it," he cried. "Now we know where to catch the damned villains. Well done, man!"

Holmes interrupted, "There is also another feature upon which you must be informed. As I have earlier told you, I made a simple sketch of the foot print that I discovered within the room in which the robbery occurred.

"Go on!" encouraged Spencer Ewart.

"Several years ago," continued Holmes," I obtained a copy of a small work, titled *Hardington's Treatise upon Naval Footwear of the World.*

The book itself, evidenced little possibility of a best seller by virtue of its title, yet I believed it to be of interest to me in my collection of possible facts."

Realising that his comments had provoked no verbal intrusion, he continued.

"Searching amongst the numerous pages of the work, I discovered the existence of a German naval boot, known as *FussSchultz dem Deutches Marines*, accompanied by a drawing of the sole of the boot that matched exactly the sketch that I had earlier made."

"Then the perpetrators of this disgusting crime are German based?" hissed Spencer Ewart.

"It would indicate so," replied Holmes. "Do you have any news upon the post mortem of the unfortunate shot outside Portsmouth?"

The other produced a sheet of paper from the file upon his desk.

"Yes!" he replied. "According to the pathologist's report, the man in question died from the effects of a bullet introduced into the cranial cavity, utterly destroying the medulla obligata and immediately rendering life extinct."

"Yes, yes, yes," remarked Holmes testily. "But what about the diameter of the bullet?"

The other glanced again at his paper.

"According to this report, the calibre of the fatal round was in measurement, 7.63 millimetres," he announced.

Holmes smacked his hand to his right leg triumphantly.

"At last!" he cried. "We may have positive proof of the identity of the originators of this foul act."

"How so?" commented Spencer Ewart.

"Because my dear fellow" exalted Holmes, "the 7.63 bullet comes from the German Mauser pistol and none other."

"Oh, come on Holmes!" ejaculated Spencer Ewart. "How can you be so certain?"

Holmes demurred for a second at the other's lack of knowledge. "If we are principally concerned in discovering which country has authorised this unwarranted assault upon our nation," he began, "then to determine the weapons, most used by the countries, the subject of our assessment, to my mind would prove most valuable."

Spencer Ewart was about to reply but Holmes waved him to silence.

"French agents would employ a weapon known as the Lebel 1892, which employs a barrel bore of 8 millimetres," he began. "If the Russians were involved, their standard pistol is the Nagant M 1895, of 7.62 calibre."

The other sat back in admiration of my colleague's intelligence. Holmes continued.

"I am now satisfied that the current situation we face, concerns the invasion of German agents into this country. Within a day or so, I expect to have more positive evidence for your edification. Until that time, I would seek your indulgence."

"Of course, Holmes," said Spencer Ewart. "But, for my own part, I need to know of your further intentions."

"Quite so," replied Holmes, "but before I reveal these, I think that we should now refer to these miscreants as agents for, it is becoming more obvious that the entire action was not the brainchild of a few disconcerted individuals but, the concerted act of a foreign power. Most possibly Germany, against the sovereignty of a friendly nation."

"You have my wholehearted agreement," replied Spencer Ewart. "But to convince our powers that be, I shall require further evidence."

"To that extent stated Holmes "I plan to travel to a small, east Suffolk village by the name of Thorpe tomorrow."

"Thorpe!" echoed Spencer Ewart. "You believe that this part of the coast is the point where these villains plan to export their evil gains?"

"Following my visit to Portsmouth and my scientific investigations upon which you have been informed," said Holmes turning to me to me, "and with the information supplied by my colleague upon possible smuggling areas, easily available, together with my knowledge of the early youth of the believed progenitor of this foul crime, I believe the same to be true."

"Then I will have the area covered by my men immediately," said Spencer Ewart. Holmes held up his hand.

"Not too fast, my dear chap," he murmured. "The birds have not arrived and there is little benefit to be obtained in ruffling their feathers."

"Then what do you propose, Holmes?" enquired the other. "For it would appear that at this moment in time, I am in your hands."

"Watson and I will take a trip to Thorpe," he began. "We shall travel to Ipswich and there take a connection to Leiston, which is but a short distance from the hamlet in question. Late last night and having assured myself that the hamlet of Thorpe is the object of our investigations, I consulted, John Murray's excellent handbooks upon traveller's Britain and discovered the existence of a small inn, by name the Crown, that lies within the hamlet concerned. We shall therefore take rooms within the same and investigate further."

Spencer Ewart appeared somewhat concerned at this. "Surely, Holmes," he began "your arrival and presence within the hamlet will arouse the interest and possible suspicion of many of its inhabitants?"

"Not at all," remarked Holmes. "We shall introduce ourselves as a couple of bird watchers bent upon the study of natural fauna, prevalent within the coastal areas."

"Bird Watchers!" exclaimed Spencer Ewart.

Holmes grinned. "Bird watchers, my dear chap. Nothing more ominous than that." he explained.

"As the coast is inundated with many of the same persuasion, our presence should elicit little concern among the native populace."

"But, I need to know upon a daily basis both your findings and your further advices," said Spencer Ewart.

"So you shall my dear fellow," replied Holmes. "A telegraph facility must be available in Leiston. I shall therefore contact you on a daily basis with any facts that we are able to determine."

The other appeared satisfied by this comment but Holmes had not finished.

"As far as your own efforts are concerned," he said. "Have you any concrete evidence upon the position of the cart that we believe contains the stolen equipment?"

The other shook his head sadly.

"My men are covering the main highways from Portsmouth," he began. "But even with the addition of members of the police throughout the counties we expect these villains to travel, I lack sufficient bodies to ensure that all routes may be staffed."

At this comment, Holmes sniffed loudly in the most contemptuous manner. "So be it!" he remarked. "Even so, we may have an element of luck upon our side."

Spencer Ewart's face lightened.

"If my calculations are correct," continued Holmes. "We may have some seven to eight days before these vile robbers make the Suffolk areas. Taking this fact into account and waiting for the correct evening tide -- for to attempt to disembark in daylight would be most foolhardy, we may add a further day or two."

"What leads you to that deduction, Holmes?"

"The robbery in question occurred precisely a week ago," continued Homes. "It is now Thursday and if my own estimation following my recent investigations and deductions are correct, we have little to concern ourselves with for the better part of the next seven days, perhaps longer. In the intervening period," he continued, "I would suggest that you place a high-speed motor gunboat within a berth in the proximity to the area of coastline that we consider any attempt at embarcation to occur. The reason for its real appearance may be concealed as a show of amity between the Royal Navy and one of its eastern harbours. I can surely leave the details up to you."

Spencer Ewart nodded. "You believe that I should order a motor gunboat to the area?" he asked somewhat timorously. "That action will surely upset the Admiralty."

Holmes actually fumed at this remark. "For goodness sake, man!" he exploded. "This is a matter vital to the continued security of this country. Instruct the same to be done or face the terrible consequences for your failure, not so to do."

Spencer Ewart appeared to physically shrivel within his chair at Holmes's outburst. "It will be as you wish, Mr. Holmes," was all he was able to mutter.

Holmes stood up and I followed his action.

Seated beside Holmes, I noted that the Head of Military Intelligence appeared to have lost the presence of power and authority he so clearly portrayed upon our initial meeting. The man virtually sagged within the confines of his chair. Weakly, he raised his arm in a gesture of acceptance. "Then, for the time, I must leave the entire issue in your hands, Holmes," he mumbled lamely.

"I will leave for Suffolk tomorrow," announced Holmes. "Having established accommodation to my liking within the hamlet of Aldringham, cum Thorpe, I will send you my first telegram by early the day after tomorrow at the latest." He turned to me.

"Come Watson," he commanded. *"Tempus Fugit!"*

Chapter Three

Liverpool Street Station, London, October, 1906

The huge iron stanchions supporting the tumbling, glazed, somewhat grimy sections of the massive roof, permitted little brilliance of the early morning sunlight to permeate through upon the multitudinous and colourful assembly that thronged the railway station below.

We had been fortunate to obtain reservations within the confines of a first-class compartment of a locomotive of medium pace that, would allow us a journey to Ipswich where a branch line would afford us further conveyance to Leiston. Apart from the normal luggage required by gentlemen set upon a few days excursion, Holmes had brought with him a briefcase, the contents of which he steadfastly refused to disclose. All he would say was, "The contents will be of value later, Watson."

Having seated ourselves comfortably, Holmes informed me that a restaurant facility was also offered by the railway company and, as the expected journey to Ipswich appeared to be in excess of an hour, offered me the opportunity to enjoy a railway breakfast.

Having dined at some of London's premier establishments and left feeling a little disappointed, I must say that I have never failed to be most impressed and contented with the catering facilities of our rail system and so, readily agreed to his suggestion. My thoughts were not misplaced.

Plump Elmswell pork sausages and dry cured back bacon, garnished with kedgeree and tomatoes of the most piquant acidity, taunted my palate in the most profligate manner, and I had completed consuming at least half my plate, before Holmes interrupted my gourmandic reverie.

"I believe that we must discover a hiding place within which these foul miscreants intend to conceal the results of their robbery," he announced. "Thus if my thoughts are correct and my deductions that Moran is the chief progenitor of what has occurred be true, some concealment would have been sought and obtained upon the coastline selected for their ingress and the egress of the stolen equipment."

I said nothing and my silence allowed me to consume the vestiges of my railway breakfast. Homes allowed me this brief period before taxing me further.

"So, what shall we do, Watson." he began."

My defence was attack. "What have you decided to do, Holmes?" I mumbled, digesting the last mouthful of kedgeree. "For your agile brain as opposed to my simple logic, has always proved successful to the cases in which we have been previously involved."

Holmes looked at me across the dining table in a most quizzical manner.

"Do I detect a degree of petulance, Watson?" he said softly.

I took a mouthful of Assam and replied, "Not at all, my dear fellow and no offence is intended. It is a proven fact that criminal detection is a field upon which you are the acknowledged champion. Please believe that any slight you may have thought I may have offered, was never meant."

He looked at me for a second then also availed himself of a draught of Assam. "Then let us return to my earlier question. What in your valued opinion, is to be our next step?"

Holmes's diplomacy was always one of his strongest and most likeable traits and I, as usual, became a willing pawn.

"If our purpose in travelling to the Suffolk coast is to determine where these stolen items might more readily be hidden before their eventual embarcation to a yet undetermined continental port? Then I believe that we should initially discover where they might readily be stored, until the arrival of their mode of transport, for unexpected conditions might delay their plans." I offered. Holmes appeared delighted with this comment.

"Capital Watson!" he practically roared. "You've hit the nail on the head."

I was initially concerned that Holmes's outburst might have interrupted the delications of the other diners within the restaurant car but upon looking about, discovered the four other inhabitants were far too concerned with their Elmswell sausages to pay us but the briefest attention.

Holmes leant across the dining table. "Then what, my dear friend, would be your next step upon our arrival at Leiston?" he demanded.

Thrilled to have been asked to suggest and action rather that to be told, I eagerly replied. "Discover what property capable of concealing the items concerned had been recently purchased," I replied.

Holmes appeared ecstatic. "Good for you, Watson! And thus our next step?"

"We seek out the services of a local land agent and enquire further," I replied.

"Exactly my dear friend," responded Holmes. "That is precisely what I would have decided upon without," he added, "your valued contribution." For some unaccountable reason, I experienced a sense of elation.

"However," continued Holmes. "We have to disguise the ultimate reason for our visit. Let us say that, apart from enjoying the pleasures of Suffolk wildlife, we also seek the possibility of acquiring a substantial coastal property, "What might be our reason for this intended purchase?" I thought for a few moments,

"We might intimate that our real purpose is to develop a part of, what is today a desolate and lonely coast into a delightful and profitable area for holiday makers," I engendered.

Holmes appeared to accept this suggestion. "Then that is what we shall present to any we might encounter," he added.

He regarded the remains of my breakfast and sighed.

"Perhaps you would kindly consume the detritus remaining of the Elmswell sausage upon your plate, Watson. I believe that we are about to enter Ipswich station."

We caught our branch line connection on the Ipswich-Yarmouth railway and arrived at Leiston station at eleven thirty.

Leiston, Suffolk, October, 1906

The railway station appeared deserted of any life apart from a rather fat, fluffy cat that sprawled, sleepily upon the slats of the only seat noticeably available within the short platform. The creature regarded our arrival with the disinterest normally shown by a Bengal tiger to a butterfly and thus, we both paid the somnambulant feline little further attention.

Holmes called for a porter and after several exhortations, a man appeared from within the confines of the small building that served as the station quarters.

"I wish to speak with your station master," said Holmes. The other looked blank at this request.

"He ain't in today," he replied.

"Why not?" enquired Holmes.

""Cos he isn't" said the other.

"Well where is he?" demanded Holmes.

"Out!" replied the other.

Holmes was bubbling for a verbal admonishment. At that point, I interceded.

"Perhaps you might be able to assist us? I enquired solicitously." It worked and the porter immediately relaxed his earlier impertinence and smiled at me.

"Always happy to oblige, sir," he responded. "And what may I do for you?"

For once, I indicated that my colleague should say nothing, and he subsided into a rather petulant silence.

"We seek the offices of a local land agent. Do you know of any?" I enquired. The porter scratched his chin.

"There is one in the High street," he murmured. "But that be the only one, as far as I know."

"Can you recall the name of this company?" said I. The porter smiled.

"Course I can," he began. "I live 'ere don't I? Now let me think for a minute. It's something like, Dick or Flick. No hang on, I've got it. Quick & Co. You can't miss them. After you leave the station, turn right into High Street, and the building you want is about a hundred yards on the left."

Our current conversation being finished to my satisfaction and having thanked the porter profusely for his instructions, I looked at Holmes who with a contemptuous nod of the head, indicated that our business at the station to his mind, was at an end and thus, we should make our exit.

The offices of Quick & Co. occupied a rather delightful "mock" Tudor building possessing an enormous bow window through which the timber glazing bars permitted the interested viewer to inspect a selection of local properties available for purchase or rent.

Upon opening the door, the gentle chimes of a small, brass bell, announced our presence. The outer office into which we entered was small and contained a desk and a cabinet used for filing important documents. A young man welcomed us and enquired upon our business and, upon hearing of its nature, disappeared for a few moments before returning to ensure us that, his employer, a certain gentleman by the name of Currel Daward, would be delighted to meet with us. Following this, we were ushered into the back room where his employer conducted his daily business.

The man that rose to meet us was tall and possessed the countenance of an individual who considers most others of a level beneath his own. How wrong might I be?

Currel Daward proved to be one of the most affable characters that I have ever encountered. His acceptance of our requirements and further, the evidence of his obvious intention to fulfil our every request, both impressed and endeared the man.

We had previously decided for the purposes of national security, that disclosure of our real names might prove detrimental to our purpose and thus, introduced ourselves as. Groves and Wilson. We stated that we were avid ornithologists and were seeking a spot where our joint interests might be better provided for. In short, we sought a section of the Suffolk coast where wildlife enjoyed predominance. This appeared to more than satisfy Currel Daward.

Holmes stated that although we were seeking to acquire a property, either by purchase or rent within the area of Thorpe, he had no idea of what properties might be available.

"What size and accommodation would you be seeking to acquire, Mr. Groves?" enquired Currel Daward.

"Enough room for both my colleague and I, my staff of let us say, of four and furthermore, outbuildings for the garaging of at least one motor vehicle replied Holmes. His next statement caught me unawares.

"My colleague is a water colourist of some note," he added. "It would be to my interest if one of the buildings upon the site that I seek, might be easily convertible into a studio. If you will permit me, I have brought with us a few samples of his latest works."

I was flabbergasted by my friend's statements. The closest artistic effort that I had ever produced was a sketch of a black cat. Whatever was Holmes thinking about? I had but little time to wait.

Delving within the confines of his briefcase, Holmes produced several rolled canvasses which he then spread out upon Currel Daward's desk.

The other bent over his desk, his eyes widened at the illustrations set before him. I looked at Holmes who returned my anxious gaze with a wink. I therefore said nothing.

"These are most excellent," he breathed. "Some of the finest interpretations of our coastline that I have ever seen."

"They are but work in progress," replied Holmes.

At this statement, Currel Daward raised his hands.

"Oh, Mr. Groves!" he announced sorrowfully. "Had you but consulted me but a few months ago, I would have been able to offer you the most perfect property suited to your requirements. Alas, it has been acquired by another."

"Artist?" enquired Holmes. Currel Daward shook his head.

"I know not," he admitted sheepishly. The negotiations for the property concerned were handled entirely by a firm of lawyers in London. In fact, since the completion of the purchase, nothing has been seen of the purchaser.

"Perhaps he has had second thoughts," said Holmes. "If this is the case, it might be possible to make a further offer for the property? May I enquire as to its exact location?" Currel Daward appeared more than ready to supply this information.

"The property in question is situated approximately equally distant between the hamlet of Thorpe and the nearby town of Aldeburgh," he stated. "The land upon which the buildings are situated is of little agricultural value, being composed of scrub and inland creeks subject to flooding by the incumbent sea. The original farm and its out buildings have suffered from the ever-present situation of coastal erosion and has become of little value to any gentleman seeking to exploit its earlier propensities."

Nevertheless," said Holmes. "I would dearly like to see the property for myself."

"And so you may, Mr. Groves," responded Currel Daward. "Perhaps upon the morrow?"

At this point, Holmes produced his gold Hunter, studied the face and replaced the same within his waistcoat.

"I am reminded that I yet must arrange accommodation for the coming night," he began. "The afternoon draws to its close."

Currel Daward rose from his chair. "My dear Groves," he said." Think no more upon your lodging this night. You appear to seek a property within the little hamlet of Thorpe, and I have a friend who occupies the only inn within the area. I will send word and your accommodation will be assured. How long do you wish to remain within our area?"

"Perhaps for two nights only upon this occasion," replied Holmes.

"Then, it shall be done," said Currel Daward. He clapped his right hand to his head.

"Of what am I thinking?" he exclaimed. "Of course, you both shall dine with me this evening. My dear wife would never rest, should she believe that I had allowed such eminent personages to leave our small town without making her acquaintance. Shall we say at seven o'clock?"

I realised that I was totally out of the current conversation and awaited Holmes's reply. I knew that he was going to refuse the invitation, but he did not.

"Your kind invitation is most readily accepted," he said. "Yet it is but four of the clock and some three hours remain before we may avail ourselves of your most generous hospitality."

Currel Daward would not be put off. "Fear not, Mr. Groves," he virtually chirruped, "my assistant shall shortly see to what must be accomplished." At that, he called out, "Esmonde!"

The young lad that had originally greeted us appeared.

"Tell Biggens that his conveyance is most urgently required to transport these two gentlemen to the Crown Hotel. Send a man to inform Sawyer that they are to be provided with his best rooms. Return yourself to the Crown Hotel around six-thirty whereupon these gentlemen will have sufficient time to address themselves for the evening and deliver them back to my house by seven o'clock. Is that clearly understood?"

Esmonde nodded nervously. "As you wish, sir," he mumbled.

Suddenly, our new host appeared somewhat nervously embarrassed.

"Do you possess white ties gentlemen?" he enquired. Holmes shook his head. "We had not thought to require the same," he confessed.

The other appeared relieved. "Then we shall dine in country fashion," he chortled happily. "I shall wear my tweed and instruct my dear wife to dress accordingly." Holmes was quick to rectify any sartorial concerns. "My dear fellow," he began, in a most affable manner, "our mode of dress is of little consequence to my mind, balanced against the obvious pleasure of the forthcoming evening with both you and your dear wife."

Currel Daward beamed happily. "Then I have little to worry about and shall content myself in looking forward to the enjoyment of a pleasant evening." Suddenly Currel Daward appeared perplexed.

"Goodness me!" he exclaimed. "I have clearly forgotten to inform my dear wife of our arrangement. What will she say upon the arrival of two guests for dinner, when she knows not of their invited presence?" Both Holmes and I remained silent.

"Esmonde!" called out our evening's host. The young lad appeared looking somewhat fatigued.

"Yes sir," he practically groaned.

Currel Daward scribbled something upon a piece of office paper, folded the same and handed it to the office junior.

"Please take this immediately to Mrs. Currel Daward and inform her that, should there be anything that she should require to substantiate this evening's meal, then she must immediately purchase the same upon my account within the local shopkeepers." Esmonde took the folded paper yet appeared to hesitate.

"Off you go, my boy!" said Currel Daward. "Be quick now!"

"The cab has arrived," said Esmonde.

"Good!" said, Currel Daward. He turned to us.

"Gentlemen, your carriage awaits. It only remains for me to look forward in pleasurable anticipation to our meeting later this evening."

Stadtschloss Palace - Berlin, May, 1906

The German Emperor smiled coldly.

"Then tell me more of this plan?" he enthused.

"The operatives employed to carry out this possible operation are, at present, undergoing intensive training, Your Majesty," replied von Schiffert.

"How do you intend to convey these men, both to and from their intended port of entrance?" enquired the Kaiser.

"A motor launch has been converted to appear as a fishing boat," stated von Schiffert. "The coastline in which we intend to land is filled with such craft. One more will attract little notice. Should our eventual departure result in the unwarranted attention of the Royal Navy, the vessel's speed will easily allow it to outdistance any other sent to intercept it."

"And these men that you have sought to employ?" enquired the Kaiser. "What of their ability and loyalty?"

"They are a mixture of disaffected European nationalities who owe little loyalty to anything other than money, my Kaiser," replied von Schiffert. "I suppose in modern terms, they would best be described as anarchists."

"But do they realise by whom they are employed/" continued the Kaiser.

"Since their original recruitment, they have been kept wholly unaware of their eventual master," replied the general. "Throughout their transport in Germany and to the site which has been specially constructed for their training, they have been totally unaware of their surroundings," stated von Schiffert. "In fact, in their estimation, they might well be in Russia or Serbia for all they know."

The German Kaiser nodded his appreciation.

"And in the impossible event that this mission fails, von Schiffert?"

"Procedures have been put in place to ensure that none of the men involved ever return to Germany, Your Majesty."

"Ah!" sighed the Kaiser. "It was as I had hoped. Whatever happens, no blame for any action must ever be levelled at Germany."

The Kaiser stood up, signifying that the audience had ended.

Von Schiffert bowed and left the chamber. He failed to hear the final words, murmured by his Kaiser.

"Even you, general, may be disposable."

For a few seconds the German Emperor surveyed his luxurious surroundings. His thoughts were interrupted by a page.

"Forgive me your Imperial Highness," announced the page. "There is a gentleman who refuses to give his name and requests an audience with you. He informs me to say that he is 99."

The Kaiser stiffened.

"Show this gentleman into a private apartment," he ordered.

Thorpe, October, 1906

The combination of the iron shod wheels of the carriage and the incessant clip-clopping of the horses' hooves prevented any conversation between Holmes and myself being either heard or understood by our cabbie.

"Whatever are you thinking, Holmes?" I began. "First to introduce me as a recognised painter and further, to place us both into a situation where our real identities may possibly be discovered?" I could not see Holmes within the confines of the darkened carriage, but I knew he was smirking.

"My dear chap," he offered. "I believe that we seek a more acceptable provenance to justify our visit to the Suffolk coast than, merely Bird Watchers or whatever those wretched individuals refer to themselves as being."

"But I know little of art," I protested weakly." What if Currel Daward's wife should ask me upon the quality and design of her own works?" Holmes chuckled within the dark confines of the creaking carriage.

"My dear chap," said my friend. "No artist of any importance will ever seek the approbation of another. If the lady concerned should require your comments, then believe me, she is but a novice." I was unconvinced and enquired further of my colleague.

"That may be so, Holmes. But how shall I answer her questions?"

"Purse your lips and murmur only of, perspective, intensity of hue and shadow," said Holmes, "And upon any further enquiry by the lady concerned, merely shake your head and whisper, "And yet, I see so much potential."

"Will that suffice?" I asked.

"More than adequately," said Holmes.

The Crown Hotel was in fact little more than an ale house with rooms.

We were cordially welcomed by the landlord who then showed us to our accommodation and having enquired as to whether we would require a meal, appeared more than satisfied that we were due to return to Currel Daward's table later that evening.

Having attired ourselves suitably and it being some minutes after the hour of six o'clock, Holmes suggested that we might retire to the house bar and avail ourselves of a small sherry before our trip back to Leiston.

Sawyer stood behind his bar and beamed at us upon our entrance into the ground floor room that served as the main bar to the alehouse.

"What can I get you, gentlemen?" he enquired.

Holmes ordered two sherries, at which the man's face fell.

"I'm sorry," he began. "But I don't have any Spanish wines within the house. May I offer you a glass of brandy instead?" Holmes sighed and nodded.

"If that is all you have, then it will suffice," he stated.

Sawyer served our drinks.

"Funny!" he stated. "You're the second gentlemen who have come in and ordered drinks that I don't stock..."

"Oh?" said Holmes. "Who were the others?"

Sawyer leant across the bar counter, his action obviously compelling our similar action. ""The gentlemen over there," he announced quietly, nodding at two youngish men, clad in working clothes, who sat at a small table in the far side of the bar.

"They come in about three weeks ago and asked me for something called Ginaver, or was it Gineater?"

Holmes interrupted him. "Was it by any chance, Ginever?" he enquired. The other's face brightened.

"That's it, Mr. Groves. That's the tipple. Well, I ain't got it so they settled for gin. Been coming in and drinking it ever since."

He winked and leant over the bar further. "I don't think that they be English. They speak kind of foreign."

I had noticed that one of the men seated in the far off table appeared to be staring in our direction and effected a kind of bow of salutation, but the fellow ignored my action and returned to his seated friend, so I mentally discarded his somewhat rude behaviour. At that precise moment, Esmonde came into the building and announced that our carriage awaited us.

Draining the vestiges of our brandy and assuring the landlord that our return would be within his permitted hours of business, we both left the pub and mounted our conveyance to Leiston.

Yet again, our short journey to Currel Daward's house permitted us a degree of privacy and although the sparse illumination within our conveyance allowed little but the shadowy outline of each other's features, I sensed a degree of mounting excitement within Holmes.

"You see Watson!" he muttered. "I was correct. Those ruffians within the corner of the place are most obviously foreign and, by their request for Ginever must be Dutch."

"Dutch, Holmes?" I queried. "I believed our opponents to be German. Am I wrong?" Holmes chuckled in the darkness.

"Foreign, Watson," he murmured. "Not from Suffolk."

Suddenly he smacked his hand down upon his knee.

"My God, Watson, I have been a fool!" he announced. "How stupid have I been?" I said nothing but awaited his next comment.

"The man, Sawyer may be able to supply us with information vital to this investigation," hissed Holmes. "And I have left the man to pursue an evening's entertainment of little value to this case. I realise that we may not without offence fail to attend our dinner invitation," he continued, "yet our time in Leiston must be curtailed."

"And how exactly do you intend to effect this, Holmes?"

"You must suffer the appearance of a possible heart attack." answered Holmes. "For goodness sake Watson, as a medical doctor, you must surely know the signs. Wait for my nod and then commence your play-act," he instructed.

Headquarters Military Intelligence, Whitehall, London, October 1906

Spencer Ewart smiled to himself as he considered the evening ahead. His work hours had been necessarily long this day and the prospect of meeting with a few close friends within the comfort of his club, a most delightful excursion from his daily problems. Initially, he failed to notice the rather short, portly gentleman that had entered his office and who now stood somewhat arrogantly before him. When he did, his smile froze.

"Well, Spencer Ewart, what news have you upon this robbery?" said the newcomer.

Admiral of the Fleet, Sir John Arbuthnot Fisher, for all his lack of stature, presented a most imposing figure. He was also the First Lord of the Admiralty and as such commanded the entire fleet of the British Empire.

A no nonsense man whose only reply to a situation that might be accomplished was, "Then why hasn't it?" was well known within the Royal Navy.

Nor was he a desk admiral. Since becoming a midshipman, his meteoric rise to his present position had afforded him active participation in many, naval engagements where his cool head and unflinching bravery were well known.

Furthermore, his tireless work in reform within both the service and the vessels that he commanded, had earned him the loyal affection of his peers and subordinates and the grudging respect of his enemies. It was Fisher that had promoted the design and construction of HMS Dreadnaught in which the robbery had occurred.

It was said that no man, other than Nelson, had done more for the service in which he served.

"Well?" blared Fisher again. "Come on man, I haven't got all night!"

"We are at present investigating the possible location where the stolen equipment might be removed from this country," the other said.

Fisher interrupted loudly. "But have we discovered where this stuff is at present?" he demanded.

"We believe that it to be somewhere between Portsmouth and the coast of East Anglia," replied Spencer Ewart,

"Hell's teeth!" exploded the First Sea Lord. "For all we know, the damned equipment may well have left the country!"

Spencer Ewart shook his head positively. "No, M'lord. From our present deductions, it may be another week or so before the stolen items arrive at any part of the coast capable of affording a mooring to any vessel large enough to accomplish a successful sea passage."

"You have confidence in the ability of your own men to produce this evidence?" enquired Fisher.

"I am not using my own officers," replied Spencer Ewart.

"Then who the devil are you using?" roared the other.

"Sherlock Holmes, M'lord," said Spencer Ewart, then added. "Upon the direct instructions of the Prime Minister."

For a few moments Fisher appeared nonplussed. Then a gleam of recollection appeared in his eyes. "I know the man," he said. "I met him some years ago at a reception, Isn't he the detective and subject of those somewhat spurious tales within that magazine?"

The other nodded, but Fisher had not finished.

"Why on earth do we need to rely upon the investigations of a civilian when, this matter is of purely naval concern?" At this statement, Spencer Ewart forgot himself completely.

"With respect, M'lord," he blurted out. "If this matter may be satisfactorily brought to conclusion, I care little whether the person responsible is," he paused seeking his next words, then continued, "a lord, knight, commoner or in fact a Billingsgate fishwife, as long as their information leads to the apprehension of these villains." The First Lord was vilified. "Damn your impertinence, sir!" he growled, and for a few moments, Spencer Ewart felt the freezing sense of the well-known Fisher stare. Then the others look melted and he smiled ruefully.

"My God man, not many speak to me as straight as you have. You're right of course. Carry on but be sure to inform me of any developments, however trivial upon which you become informed." The First Sea Lord glanced at the wall clock upon the wall behind Spencer Ewart's desk and grimaced.

"My God!" he muttered. "I'm going to be late. I shall be in more trouble than if I mistakenly ordered the entire fleet to the Antarctic on a summer cruise."

Spencer Ewart suddenly realised that the First Sea Lord was wearing full white tie and tails.

"M'lord is due to attend a banquet?" he offered.

"God no!" exclaimed the other. "Worse than that. My wife has organised a ball somewhere in Mayfair at which I am supposed to be principal guest. I fear that I am already late."

"But your lordship is well known for his proficiency in the dance," began Spencer Ewart.

"Impertinence in moderation, I will accept," retorted the First Sea Lord. "However, sycophancy in any form, I will never, sir."

"I meant no offence," replied the other. "Yet, your instruction to your officers when visiting foreign ports to encourage dances aboard ship where the junior officers may avail themselves in dancing with local ladies has proved most popular, both with the officers involved and more importantly, with the local inhabitants of the ports concerned."

"In that observation you are correct," said Fisher. "It was an idea that appears to have worked." Suddenly his face fell and he raised his eyes to the ceiling of the room. "God forbid!" he mused, "that I ever extend my invitation to the ratings within my warships. A few tots of rum and the sight of a pretty bosom might result in an international incident."

The First Lord made to leave the room then half turned to Spencer Ewart and waggled a rather pudgy finger.

"Don't forget," he admonished severely. "I must be informed, immediately you receive any further information on this matter!"

Currel Daward's house, Leiston, October, 1906

As is often the case, expectations of little are overshadowed by provisions of excellence.

The table gleamed with the reflected glory of silver cutlery and delicate Meissen plate, beneath the glow of two silver candelabra.

Mrs. Currel Daward was most effusive in her welcome. A charming lady, nearing middle age and of the round proportions both in face and form, that suited and moreover was expected of her position within the local community. Currel Daward himself allowed us the time to introduce ourselves to his dear wife before announcing that dinner was about to be served.

The set of the table should have told me that our coming repast would be out of the normal and this proved to be so.

Native oysters squatting within greenery and sliced lemon reposed upon a huge silver platter that but shortly became vacant upon our avaricious attention.

Following this, a huge haunch of venison was brought to the table, followed by bowls of potatoes, sliced beans and two pots of a most delicious gravy.

Decanted wines prohibited knowledge of their origin yet, both the fresh, crisp white and the heavy, full bodied red, announced our host's palate for some of the most noted vineyards.

Whereas, Holmes spent most of the meal in deep conversation with Currel Daward, I was treated to an unending discourse by his wife.

Having readily taken me into her confidence, she embarked upon possibly more private details of both her marriage and her husband's family.

She had married her husband without the blessing of her husband's parents, who considered the matrimonial match far beneath his station. Their initial objections had been rectified to the acceptance of all but, their original objections had stirred her emotions to a point where she had actively sought to explore the antecedents of the Currel Daward family.

"Whereas the discovery of a skeleton within the family cupboard is most interesting, Mr. Wilson," she whispered conspiratorially. "I have unearthed a virtual cupboardful."

As a gentleman, I gently advised the dear lady that my status prohibited my enquiries into her further discoveries, but she would have none of it. She pointed her finger at her husband and continued.

"His mother, upon her deathbed, informed the family that her parents had yet to be wed upon the time of her conception," she continued. "What do you make of that, Mr. Wilson.?" I averred any comments upon my own behalf and looked at Holmes. At that precise moment he looked at me and winked, which was our agreed sign. I returned my attention to Mrs. Currel Daward.

Now was my turn.

I grimaced and clutched my chest.

"Whatever is the matter, Mr. Wilson?" exclaimed the dear lady. "Have you indigestion?"

I shook my head. "I fear an onset of my angina," I winced and fumbled for an imaginary pill within my waistcoat and popped nothing into my twisted mouth.

"Shall we summon the attendance of a doctor?" enquired my hostess.

"No!" I winced again. "Yet I fear that I must insist upon my return to my bed where a good night's rest will surely settle my problem."

"Then you must reside here," insisted my hostess. This was the last thing that both I and Holmes required but how might I redress the situation? Holmes came to the rescue.

"My dear lady," he began. "I am well used to my friend's bouts of this nature and do assure you that, with a good night's rest, he will be himself again. Unfortunately, the nature of his illness requires both peace and quiet and a return to the stillness that may be found at our hotel. Remaining here within the company which has excited the onset of his present condition, may well prove most injurious to his health. Thus, with your permission and my sincere thanks for such an excellent evening, I am forced to insist upon a carriage to return us to Thorpe.

Upon this, Currel Daward solicitously sent for Esmonde and shortly thereafter, we found our way back upon the road to our hotel.

Again, the incessant clatter of horses' hooves and the

iron shod wheels of the conveyance permitted some brief, un-overheard conversation.

"So what did you discover, Holmes?" I enquired. Although I was unable to discern his form, his voice was exultant.

"That man, Currel Daward was a positive source of information." he declared.

"By the way," he continued," your act this night ranks with the performance of our most accepted actor upon the current stage. It was brilliant."

Accepting this accolade, I enquired further. "So what did you discover?" said I.

"According to Currel Daward, the property that has been so recently acquired by unknown others was at one time a successful agricultural holding," replied Holmes.

"However, due to incursion by the sea, the land became of little agricultural value and the then-owner, rather than selling up at a most incautious value, decided to transform the dwelling into a business able to cater for the wishes of the fishing industry."

"What was that?" said I.

"The treatment of freshly caught fish." replied Holmes.

"Treatment! What treatment?" I enquired somewhat rashly. I sensed a snigger from Holmes within the darkened confines of our conveyance.

"Kippers!" he answered. "Herring has to be smoked before it becomes the delicacy you so admire, my dear friend. The failed agricultural holding became a smokery for various types of fish, believed more edible after their immersion within the fumes of certain burnt woods."

"Much as I enjoy a good kipper, Holmes," I remarked. "I hardly see just how the fact of an old smokery might add to our present investigations." At this and although I was unable to hear the same, I imagined Holmes sighed deeply before his next words.

"My dear Watson, the presence of a disused shed would allow the concealment of the items which we seek," he began. "What I have this night learned from our jovial host Currel Daward, makes me more certain that this tiny hamlet is the exact place upon which our investigations should be set."

"How may you be so certain?" I enquired.

"Currel Daward also informed me that the previous owner obtained permission for the erection of a timber jetty that projected from the beach and some yards into the sea to afford local fishing smacks berthing before discharging their catch to the smoking shed," replied Holmes. "The now disused jetty provides a perfect structure for a shallow draught vessel at high tide to take on board the items so recently stolen. I need to speak some more with the landlord upon our return."

We spoke no more until we arrived back at the Crown and having thanked Esmonde profusely for his service, made our way into the hotel.

The bar was empty and lit only by a few candles. Of Sawyer, there was little sign, and we were welcomed by a rather plain girl who introduced herself as Jenny and explained that Sawyer had been unavoidably obliged to leave the hotel but, instructed her to provide us with such service we might require.

She had little further information to supply and willingly served us a large brandy before we retired to our rooms for the night.

Schorfheide, Germany, Late September, 1906

Moran permitted a smug smile of satisfaction as the shadowy figures executed his training instructions to the letter.

The men had been well-chosen and though of different nationalities, blended perfectly into a team capable of obeying an order without concern to its effects.

Shortly, they would move secretly to a specially prepared section of the recently constructed dockyard at Kiel where a facsimile of the Portsmouth dockyard had be constructed to precise detail. There they would practice their assault upon the British base.

They had been with him now for some five months and were now at their peak fitness. Moran's single concern was of how to control a body of men trained for action, in a state or readiness without action.

Following their visit to Kiel, they would leave for a secret destination where they would be afforded luxuries and the companionship of certain *ladies* until the mission commenced within the following seven days.

He had little concerns upon, O'Malley and Rourke. As Feinians, their historical hatred of the British, ranked alongside his own.

The others were a mixture of European dissidents who

for some reason or another, owed their loyalty to the amount of money that they expected to receive. They, unlike the Irish, required more attention if the mission planned, were to succeed.

Stadtschloss Palace, Berlin, September, 1906

"I have heard little from you, Herr General," stated the Kaiser. "What is the current situation?"

"From the Englishman leading this squad, I understand that their basic training is now at an end. They move to Kiel tomorrow."

The Kaiser appeared puzzled. "Kiel?" he said. "Why Kiel?"

For von Schiffert, the answer was simple.

"It is well known that Your Majesty has ordered the expansion of this principal dockyard," he began. "What is unknown by all inquisitive onlookers is, within their current building programme, our builders are constructing a perfect copy of the naval dockyard in Portsmouth. This will permit any team that we may send into Britain, to have extensive knowledge of the area in which they will operate."

"Ah!" murmured the German Emperor." Then there is little left to chance?"

Von Schiffert permitted himself an indulgent smile.

"Nothing, your Majesty." he replied. "Our success is guaranteed."

"Good!" remarked the Kaiser. Then I look forward to our next meeting."

Von Schiffert bowed and left the chamber.

For a few seconds, the Kaiser remained seated within his imperial chair then, he stood up.

"Why are my generals too often concerned with only success when failure may be its ultimate bedfellow," he muttered.

Thorpe, Suffolk, October, 1906

An intensely bright, sunlit shard of an October morning sought the single crack within the unclosed section of my curtains and moved unchecked across the counterpane to settle itself upon my sleeping eyelids. I was awake in an instant and knowing my friend's propensity for little sleep, arose and dressed myself for an early breakfast.

Upon reaching the trestle that served as the breakfast table, I found Holmes already seated and well past his first cup of tea.

Of Sawyer, there appeared little further sign, and it was Jenny who attended to our breakfast of Suffolk bacon, sausages and eggs.

When Jenny was without our dining area and there being no one else within the room, Holmes, having first satisfied that we were alone, leant across the small table and began.

"We must leave this place as soon as we can, Watson. To this extent, I have settled our account and discovered that a train leaves Leiston for Ipswich at midday. Our connection is due to arrive at Liverpool Street, at the latest by three this afternoon. I wish to be at Military Headquarters no later than four."

""If urgency is paramount," I offered "then why may not we leave now?" Holmes shook his head.

"We must afford ourselves a short walk upon the coast." he stated. "I need to see this farm and its outbuildings, not forgetting the jetty, for myself. As such, you will bring with us your binoculars so, to all intents, we are but bird watchers within a known bird haven." He cast an eye about again then continued. "I am more than concerned by the disappearance of our host, the landlord," he continued. "No one appears to have a plausible reason for his absence, and I believe that he may be able to provide invaluable information to our current investigation." He regarded my half full plate and grimaced. "For goodness sake, Watson, hurry up and finish that mess!" he ejaculated.

The Crown Hotel was situated some hundred yards or so from the beach, so it took us but little time to reach the same. A small road, following the coastline, led upon the right to the town of Aldeburgh. Between Thorpe and this community little but scrub, ditch and beach existed.

Upon an October morn, even accepting the prevailing sunshine, the area evidenced a sense of lonely desolation.

The path upon which we stood was more of a track than a road. To our right, the occasional tuft of sea scrub bisected the sand that dipped to the cold waters of the North Sea and led in a gentle curve to the barely discernible roofs of the town of Aldeburgh.

The farm that we sought was easily discernible upon

the barren outlook, as was the jetty upon the desolate beach. A single track led from the path upon which we walked to the farm itself.

Holmes insisted that we walk some way past the farm and was incredibly propitious in his use of the binoculars. Stopping to point at this or that, which he could not even see. However, to a casual viewer, his manner must have been totally acceptable.

We had stopped some distance from the entrance to the farm and Holmes lit his pipe.

"Of any semblance of occupation or in fact life, I can see nothing, Watson." he remarked. "Yet I am sure that both those men whom we saw in the hotel bar last night, perhaps even more, are within that farmhouse."

"Then what do propose that we should do now, Holmes?" I enquired.

He thought for a second and looked at a ditch. "Flush 'em out with interest," he commented. I stared nonplussed by this comment. Holmes continued. "When you're after game," he explained. "There is nothing more intriguing to your quarry than knowing you are there but seeing that you are not. In its interest of your whereabouts it will forget its natural caution and more often than not betray its presence."

He looked at me and realising that I had precisely scant idea upon which he spoke, he patted my shoulder. "Render me a small service my dear friend," he began. "I shall explain all later."

"Ask what you will," I replied, wholly mystified

"Walk ahead of me some hundred yards or so," commanded Holmes. He nodded in the direction of a nearby ditch. "I shall endeavour to conceal myself within the confines of that depression and await what I believe will shortly occur."

I did as instructed and had made some one hundred and fifty yards along the road leading back to Thorpe before my friend rejoined me. He appeared most excited.

"They are there, Watson!" he growled triumphantly. "I knew it to be so and now I have proof. Noticing that you were alone, the scoundrels sought to discover my whereabouts and came outside their hiding place. I saw two, possibly three who seeking to allay their concern as to my disappearance, showed themselves to my binoculars."

Holmes patted the cased spyglasses. "We've seen enough in this hamlet," he murmured. "It is time that we made our way as quickly as possible to London."

Holmes set a brisk pace. What then occurred was entirely my own fault in having consumed more than my normal intake of breakfast tea. My problem had originated within my time in the Indian sub-continent and had steadfastly remained with me unchecked. I needed to pass water and more to the point, immediately. I informed Holmes of my imminent desire. He was most irritated.

"For goodness sake, Watson, you occasionally become so tiresome," he grumbled. "If you must go, then find a ditch where unseen, your action will not result in a summons for public indecency at the local magistrate's court."

I moved to a hollow where I believed my actions would not be overseen.

The feeling occasioned by the immediate relief of my medical abnormalities, obliterated any normal appreciation of my current surroundings. About to re-address myself, I saw it.

"Holmes!" I cried hoarsely. Holmes, come here quickly!"

The agitated face of my colleague appeared over the ditch in which I stood and suddenly lost its former appearance.

Some few feet from where I had so casually passed water, the sightless, glazed eyes and bloated features of Sawyer, floated within residual mire of the ditch.

"Leave him!" said Holmes.

"But...," I began.

"Leave him, Watson," echoed Holmes. "There is nothing in this world that we can do for the poor fellow and for the life of us, we cannot be involved. The local police will discover him. It is their problem. It now becomes a matter of the utmost importance that we reach London at our earliest opportunity."

Knowing that Holmes's mind would be a virtual cauldron of thoughts and deductions, I avoided any further conversation until, upon a few minutes into our connection to London, he suddenly turned to me and offered the prospect of some light refreshment within the restaurant car.

Holmes ordered a pot of tea and some biscuits and we both waited until after the attendant had complied with this request and departed. At last, Holmes leant across the small table that bisected our seating and spoke quietly.

"I am now wholly convinced that our visit to Thorpe or more particularly the farm and jetty is the exact location where these vile creatures intend to embark with their stolen gains," he announced. "The murder of Sawyer, for I am further convinced that his death was in no way accidental, indicates that these robbers are without mercy and will stop at nothing to conceal their foul purpose from any who they feel might frustrate this deed."

"Will not Sawyer's death involve criminal investigation by the local police force and thus incur the presence of several police officers, which must be the last thing that these villains require?" I enquired.

Holmes shook his head. "Sawyer's corpse may lay undiscovered for the next day or so," he began. "How many people investigate dykes? Your call of nature was most propitious. If discovered, it will possibly be assumed that he took an evening stroll, lost his footing and tumbled into the water-filled ditch in which he drowned. A coroner will be obliged to pronounce his official cause of death, but I doubt whether the local constabulary will be otherwise alerted. No! I believe that his killers believe themselves to be safe from discovery."

"So what is our next move?" I enquired.

"To Whitehall, where with the assistance of Spencer Ewart, we may devise a plan to thwart these specimens," replied Holmes.

Chapter Four

Thickly wooded area, Hertfordshire, October, 1906

The wagon appeared suitably camouflaged within the selected wood and the dray horses munched contentedly within their forage bags as the first streaks of dawn creased the sky. Cladding the iron-cased wheels of the wagon in leather bindings and the horses' hooves in sacking had allowed the near silent passage of the group to the point at which they now resided. The men sat about and mumbled continuously to each other, as they consumed the last vestiges of the cold cooked chicken, within the early morning chill.

Moran stood apart from the assembled gathering and considered his progress. The theft of the stolen equipment had been accomplished with an ease that he had wished for but never considered possible. He had spent several weeks selecting the route to be taken after the robbery and his choice appeared to have been accurate.

It had taken longer to reach his present position than he had calculated, yet his men and their load remained undetected. It was a good sign, There remained the journey through Hertfordshire and into Essex, after which, the Suffolk coast would be an easy step to achieve and this fact, caused a shiver of excitement to course through his frame.

He allowed himself a brief moment of pleasure. Sebastian Moran, outcast from the country that he so dearly detested, had fooled them all. Within a matter of days he would be back in Germany. It was there that his full potential would be not only realised but valued. He thought of the honours that a grateful Kaiser might decide to bestow upon one that had given him such benefit. A glorious future within his newly adopted country appeared more than a possibility.

Suddenly, his thoughts were interrupted by a cry of surprise that came from the edge of the clearing which he had chosen as his camp for the coming day. Making his way over in the direction of the outcry, Moran saw that a stranger struggled within the grasp of one of his men.

On closer investigation, the stranger bore the attire and demeanour of a common poacher and the brace of pheasants that swung from a string in his right hand confirmed this fact. The man himself, evidenced a state of fright and as Moran drew near.

"I ain't what you think I am, sir," he babbled and raising the two birds in his hand continued. "I found these laying dead on the ground. Honest, I did. You won't tell no one will you sir?"

The early morning light allowed the other to see Moran's features and his current anxiety dissipated at seeing the slight smile that stole across Moran's face.

"Rest assured my dear fellow," said Moran, placing his left hand affectionately upon the shoulders of the poacher. "Whatever your purpose within these woods, its real intent will always remain our secret."

Drawing a long knife from within the confines of his trousers' waist band, he thrust the nine-inch blade deep into the chest of the other. The poacher's eyes widened in shock then glazed in death as Moran withdrew the wicked blade, wiped of the blood and replaced the weapon within his waistband.

It was all over within the space of a few moments, causing the other men to gape at the speed of its execution. Moran however, was totally in command.

Take him deeper into the wood and bury him, he commanded. "He is a man of little account and should not be missed by any for several days. By which time, we shall be well away from here."

Several of the men picked up the lifeless corpse and made off into the depths of the wood. A Dutchman and a man called Pierre remained within the clearing.

"Do we need to move?" enquired Pierre.

Moran shook his head. "Where to?" he said. "We are committed to remain undetected within the daylight hours and thus forced to remain here until nightfall."

"But the man may be missed." said Pierre. "What if a search party is sent to discover his possible whereabouts?"

"The man was a poacher, generally regarded as unnecessary vermin by the owners of large estates within this country," began Moran. "In England, land owners consider every twig, leaf and living creature within their lands as their personal and valued property. The departure of this man from this world might even be considered an act worthy of applause, rather than criminal."

"But the police forces?" enquired Pierre. "Surely the man's family will advise them of his disappearance?"

Again, Moran shook his head.

"If the man actually has a family, they will be inured to the occasions when he is away for certain periods and, will possibly never think of informing the authorities of his absence for at least a few days. No! I believe that our concealment is secure for the coming night, after which time, we shall be well away from this area."

"Are you sure?" said Pierre.

Moran glared at the other. "Am I not responsible for the total planning and execution of this entire enterprise," he hissed. "I am never wrong!"

Unknown to Moran, he had committed a most grievous error of judgement for, had he and the assembled men paid more attention to their surroundings than the lifeless body upon the ground, they would have noticed a nearby bush from within the leafy depths of which, a pair of shocked eyes had witnessed the murder.

They would also have noticed a slight rustle as the shadowy form of another man, cautiously back-tracked through the dense undergrowth and speedily made his way from the bloody scene.

Whitehall, October, 1906

"Whatever are you staring at, Watson?" grunted Holmes irritably.

"I thought that I saw a Goldfinch," said I, pointing to one of the trees that graced the mall magnificently.

I had been pleasantly engaged by the gentle drumming of our horses' hooves upon the wet surface of the capital's principal roadway, when I had noticed the presence of the little bird.

"For goodness sake, Watson," said my companion. "We have far more important matters to contend with than the singular existence of a sparrow."

"It wasn't a sparrow. It was a goldfinch," said I, but Holmes shushed me to silence. I looked out of the window again but the little bird had flown.

Military Intelligence, Whitehall, October, 1906

Spencer Ewart appeared both concerned and perplexed.

"So what have you been able to deduce, Holmes," he enquired irritably. "You seem to have been absent for an interminable period."

"Only for the time that I informed you I would require to complete certain investigations," replied Holmes.

"And have you?" said the other. Holmes regarded the finger nails upon his right hand and appeared satisfied with what he saw. He then replied. "From my visits to both Portsmouth and Suffolk, I am sure that I now know exactly where the stolen articles are to be dispatched from this country. I am certain that Thorpe, a small hamlet upon the Suffolk coast, is where these villains will attempt to export their gains."

Spencer Ewart relaxed physically and even attempted a brief smile.

"Good!" he breathed. "The First Lord has been giving me a rough time since our last meeting. May I assure him that your deductions are correct?"

Holmes gave the other a long stare. "You may inform his Lordship, the Prime Minister, even His Majesty the King himself that my deductions, when presented by me, are never wrong," he stated somewhat arrogantly.

"You must forgive my impatience, Holmes," said the other, in a most submissive manner. "My position affords me little by concern upon a daily basis."

"I am happy to learn that the same be true," Holmes stated. "For it to be otherwise, would greatly concern me that the overall security of this country, is in the hands of a contented man."

Spencer Ewart flushed crimson. "Have a care, sir! You overstep yourself."

"My dear chap," replied Holmes affably. "You rise too quickly to gobble the bait which was never intentionally offered. I meant no offence to either you or the office that you occupy. If you found so, then I unreservedly offer my sincere apologies."

Spencer Ewart calmed down immediately. "Forgive me, Holmes. This current problem has created the most extreme pressures from sources who require answers and I for one, am unable to provide the information that they require. That is I why, I look to you."

"Then you may seek no further, sir," replied Holmes. "I

am able to tell you where exactly the villains may be apprehended and further, soon inform you upon the date when their eventual capture may be attained."

Spencer Ewart sank back into his chair. "Thank you Holmes," he murmured.

Yet my colleague had not finished.

"Have you any information yourself upon the present whereabouts of these miscreants?" Holmes asked.

"I believe that I may have," replied Spencer Ewart. "I have just received a communication from my sources in Hertfordshire that, a local poacher was foully murdered in a local wood by unidentified assailants. The information comes from another poacher who accompanied the murdered man and who witnessed the deed."

"What else did this man evidence?" hissed Holmes.

"Little other than the fact that there were several others at the spot and that he saw a large wagon parked within the clearing where the crime was committed." Holmes appeared satisfied by this.

"Good! Then we now know exactly how far these miscreants have travelled." said Holmes. "If my deductions are correct, we shall be able to apprehend these villains and recover the stolen equipment, within five days at most."

"But can we not achieve this action earlier?" enquired Spencer Ewart. "The First Sea Lord is insisting on positive action upon our part, as soon as possible."

Holmes sat back in his chair, his features set.

"It is obvious that these people care little for the sacrifice of life," he began. "Therefore any attempt to frustrate their current ambition, should be undertaken only where human habitation is basically absent. The site that I believe will be employed lays equidistant between the hamlet of Thorpe and the town of Aldeburgh. It is an isolated area within which, any use of weaponry by either side should not endanger the lives of innocent civilians.

To attempt to apprehend these people sooner and within areas of population, might involve the deaths of others whose injuries might not easily be explained."

"I see," murmured Spencer Ewart. "So what action do you propose?"

"It depends entirely upon the licence of action that you have been afforded," replied Holmes.

"Be assured, my dear Holmes," replied the other, "I enjoy the support of both the First Sea Lord and the Prime Minister, to take what action I deem necessary, as long as the final result avoids any repercussions either politically or militarily with any European country overly friendly to this nation."

"Good!" said Holmes. "Then let us concern ourselves with how this matter might be successfully concluded."

Stadtschloss, Berlin, September 1906

The remains of a white spotted, black bow tie sagged as a flag at half-mast below the voluminous folds of the thick neck.

The crumpled, ill-fitting suit, shouted earlier times of sartorial glory.

If any saving grace might be attributed to the small, bald yet powerfully built individual who sat patiently upon the only chair within the small chamber, it was his, polished patent leather shoes that gleamed brightly within the reflected electrical illumination of the room.

Herbert Kroller was a man of little account or interest to the German public.

Born in Hamburg of a father that he never knew and a mother who cared little for her infant and who regularly sold herself for a few pfennigs to supplement her daily alcoholic requirement, he had cared little, when upon her murder by a drunken "client," he had been placed within the confines of an orphanage at the tender age of three.

The spartan life, lacking the infusion of family love, had created a monster with a psychopathic hatred of the world in which he lived and by the time he was eighteen years of age, he had already, happily murdered his first three victims.

His activities had come to the attention of the Kaiser when presented with a petition of clemency, following Kroller's conviction and death sentence upon the murder of a member of the Reichstag government.

The Kaiser had scant thoughts upon the life of

individual subjects and was about to dismiss the petition when a thought entered his mind.

As German Emperor, he enjoyed dominance and respect within the German army. However in the world of politics, he had many adversaries who believed in government by the people, rather than his autocratic control. These individuals might be dangerous to his rule. Their daily actions were never treasonable, more troublesome. With a man like Kroller, owing his entire existence to the whim of his emperor, anything might be possible.

The Kaiser sighed and with a stroke of his pen, dismissed the petition.

As a matter of record, a prisoner registered by name as, Herbert Kroller was executed by guillotine in Berlin's Moabit prison on, 23rd. October, 1900.

Shortly following this event, a small man arrived at the Kaiser's hunting lodge in Romintem, East Prussia. To all existing staff, he was to be known as an *UnterJagtMeisster* to the vast estate. The newcomer was given a small lodge away from the main house and any contact by other servants was expressly discouraged, due, it was said, to the man's own preference for privacy.

Rarely seen by others, the only real evidence of the man's existence came from a servant girl picking mushrooms within the vast forests that encompassed the estate.

"He was little and had a huge bald head," she informed the other servants.

As the Kaiser entered the chamber, the other stood up and perfected a deep bow. The German Emperor waved him back to his seat.

"I have a certain matter that may require your attention," he began. "The matter in question, if occurring, may afford me a most compromising situation within which I must not be associated."

"Rest assured, you will not be, my Kaiser," replied Herbert Kroller.

Cavendish, Suffolk, October, 1906

The massive oak timbers of the barn crouched, covetously above the assembled men. It was obvious to anyone that the structure had not been used for several years. Of general accoutrements there were none. The entire structure was empty apart from the straw.

Moran sat upon one of the remaining bales of hay and considered his progress.

They had reached the county of Suffolk without hindrance and the way to the coast, but a matter of two days at most. His original plan appeared to be succeeding but, why had it all been so simple to accomplish?

"Yes!" screamed his agile brain. "It's been too easy. The British government would not give up a product that might ensure their mastery of the seas so meekly and without recourse to an attempt to recover the same. Yet, no official representation had been either seen or encountered. Whatever were they about?"

His own men were well-equipped to deal with any

incursion into their own efforts. All had been provided with semi-automatic pistols and the latest *Gewehr,* breech loading, magazine rifles and their intensive training in Germany, assured that, in unarmed combat, they were bound to prevail against any assailants. Yet, something was wrong.

His current thoughts were interrupted by the offer of a steaming cup of coffee which effectively broke his train of thought.

The brew was most satisfying, comforting and relaxing and following its consumption, Moran allowed his tiredness to assume control of his mental senses and sank into an untroubled sleep.

Headquarters Military Intelligence, Whitehall, October, 1906

"So we know the time and day," said Spencer Ewart. "What operation do you suggest that I effect to apprehend these robbers?

"Nothing that might appear overt," replied Holmes. "What have been your thoughts?"

"At least a company of regular soldiers," replied the other. "We can capture the villains before they reach their base in Suffolk."

Holmes shook his head. "The men that we face are ruthless and quite possibly well-armed," he said. "Any attempt to apprehend them may well involve an exchange of gunfire, in which innocent civilians may be killed or injured. This fact in itself will provoke enquiry into a matter that you wish to be kept secret."

"Then what do you propose?" said Spencer Ewart.

"Let us await their arrival in Thorpe," said Holmes. "Then, and only then, we make our move."

"And what might that be?" said the other. "For you must have some idea upon just how these villains might be more easily apprehended?"

"I do indeed," replied Holmes. "My first consideration concerns the protection of the innocent bystander. Upon this decision and accepting that there may well be possibly six or seven miscreants to deal with, I believe that a somewhat smaller team than a company of infantry is all that will be required to complete the action successfully. Perhaps a squad of trained yeomen, accompanied by a Maxim machine gun will suffice. I believe that our best advantage will be an attack upon the farmhouse where the villains believe themselves to be safe. The action will have to be coordinated with a high tide for, without this, any vessel sent to collect the stolen items will be unable to dock at the readily available jetty.

I further believe that if unhindered, the robbers will arrive at Thorpe within the next two or three days at the latest. As they will wish to be away with their ill-gotten gains at the earliest opportunity, I have taken the trouble to review the time table of the local tides for the next few days, and the best possible tide to suit their nefarious purposes, occurs upon the night, three days hence. I think we may assume that this date is the time that they have set for their meeting with the craft sent to complete their vile purposes."

"You mentioned the inclusion of a Maxim gun," said

Spencer Ewart. "Where do you intend to site this prodigious weapon whose firepower is readily accepted to be disastrous and often uncontrolled in its ability to kill or injure others, not the subject of its original purpose?"

"I have studied the beach surrounding the jetty," replied Holmes. "From the high-tide waterline, the entire area slopes quickly to a much higher situation, allowing any spent bullets to find their eventual target within the sandy slopes and not proceed further into a further area in which they might cause harm to another. As long as the weapon is sighted at chest high at its greatest elevation, little extraneous damage can be foreseen."

"And where would you site this awful weapon?" enquired Spencer Ewart.

"Perhaps a hundred yards from the jetty and several yards from the high water mark, where it will be invisible from that spot yet able to deliver its lethal load if required," replied Holmes.

"I believe your reasoning and plan, if applied to be most effective," said the other. Yet there is one facet that I think you have overlooked."

"Pray inform me?" said Holmes.

"How do we transport a squad of soldiers into Suffolk without arousing the suspicions of not only the local populace but the villains as well?"

"As our proposed assault is scheduled to commence around midnight upon the day in question, I see little difficulty," replied Holmes. "With sufficient advance information, it may well be possible to transport the required men from Colchester to Aldeburgh by automotive conveyance, during the afternoon prior to their eventual deployment.

"A venue must be sought to accommodate the men before their actual use is required," said Holmes.
"That is at present to subject of our current researches," replied Spencer Ewart.
"There must be no chance of any information of their existence reaching other, unfriendly ears," added Holmes.
The other appeared ruffled by this remark. "My dear Holmes," he flustered. "The service that I command relies upon its ability for secrecy."
"From what I am given to understand, my dear chap, governmental secrecy may be equated with the banal ramblings of a Middleborough washer-woman on a Monday morning."
He suddenly stopped and turned to me. "Why did I say Middleborough, Watson?" he pondered.
I shook my head. "I have no idea," I replied. "Do you know any?"
"No!" replied Holmes blankly. "My God!" he added, I hope that none of the dear ladies of that fine town ever learn of my remark."

Spencer Ewart had risen from his chair. His face nearing comparison with the red blotting paper upon his desk. Holmes immediately became all charm again. "My dear chap, do compose yourself. I meant no personal slight. I am sure that your department enjoys the highest levels of national sanctity. I refer only to other, shall we call them 'leakages' from other governmental departments, that have been referred to within the newspapers and which as you may well understand, tend to cause a blight upon the whole.?" Spencer Ewart visibly calmed at these words and sat down.

"So what are you actually saying?" enquired the other quietly.

"Winning a battle depends upon three provisions," said Holmes. "Intelligence as to your enemy's disposition and strength, a commander's own belief of what the other may or may not do, upon what he may or may not do himself and finally, a degree of luck."

Spencer Ewart was about to say something but Holmes waved him to be silent. Holmes continued.

"I shall visit Thorpe again tomorrow to conduct a thorough survey of both the farm and the surrounding land and then return to London to inform you of my findings. If my final deductions are correct," he stated, "Moran, for I truly believe it is he, will arrive at Thorpe no earlier than next Saturday and no later than next Sunday." Holmes fumbled within his coat and produced a crumpled sheet of paper at which he looked.

"Ah!" he cried. "High tide on Saturday is scheduled for 10.45 p.m. High tide on Sunday an hour and ten minutes later."

He turned to Spencer Ewart triumphantly. "Your men must be in position and ready to commence their assault upon the farmhouse by no later than, 8 o'clock on Saturday night."

Spencer Ewart scribbled some notes upon a sheet of white paper that lay upon his desk and looked up at Holmes.

"Anything else?" he enquired somewhat sarcastically.

"Yes!" replied the other.

"I have decided that my operational base should be situated in the nearby town of Aldeburgh. To station myself in the tiny hamlet of Thorpe might well attract unwelcome attention.

"Tomorrow I will travel to Aldeburgh and obtain rooms for the space of two night's accommodation.

"To avoid any suspicion, both Watson and I will identify ourselves as marine biologists, seeking exploration of the East Anglian coasts. That in itself should allay any suspicion upon the true intent of our visit.

"It will therefore be necessary for you to find secure accommodation for the officer and men that you intend to employ to complete the apprehension of these villains, within that vicinity. Are you able to effect this?"

Spencer Ewart nodded perfunctorily. ""It will be done," he murmured.

"Good!" replied Holmes. "Now, as far as our direct means of communication is concerned, I will avail myself of the services of the Aldeburgh telegraph office. From there, I will be able to inform you of the situation as it develops."

"That will be most acceptable," said Spencer Ewart. "I suggest that for security's sake, our further communications should be made in rather obtuse form. You may refer to the entire operation as "Seaweed".

"Understood," replied Holmes.

"Upon successful completion of the planned assault and recovery of the items in question, your further telegraph should read, 'Seaweed no longer a problem'," said the other.

"If the entire operation fails?" remarked Holmes.

"Then, God help this nation," replied the other glumly.

At this precise moment, the door to Spencer Ewart's office was flung open and the First Lord of the Admiralty entered and advanced upon Spencer Ewart in a most alarming manner.

"Well?" he glowered. ""What's happened and, where are we at?"

The newcomer had totally ignored both Holmes and I and we remained quietly seated within our chairs. Spencer Ewart rose from his seat and meekly indicated our presence.

"My Lord," he stammered "perhaps I might be allowed to introduce you to Sherlock Holmes and his colleague, Doctor Watson. Their assistance has been most invaluable to this current matter."

"Jackie" Fisher turned to fix us both with his well known stare.

"Holmes!" he mused then his features broke into a most appreciable beam.

"My dear chap, I failed to notice you upon my entrance. Pcasc forgive my incorrigible behaviour." Fisher looked again closely at Holmes. "My God! Man, I know you, don't I?

Holmes grinned.

"We met, my Lord, at a small soiree some years ago."

"Of course we did. I recall the exact occasion." replied the First Sea Lord. "You were trying to get me to introduce a detective element into my navy."

"And you, My Lord, informed me that I was talking the most abominable twaddle." replied Holmes. Fisher was up for this rebuke.

"My dear chap, I am more often than not, far too hasty for my own good. Please forgive any unpleasantness I may have caused you upon the occasion that we last met."

Fisher turned back to Spencer Ewart. "Well man, what do we have to go upon?

Briefly, Spencer Ewart recounted the current situation including our earlier discussions upon what might be effected at Thorpe. The First Sea Lord waited patiently until after he had finished.

"So it's agreed," he stated. "The entire 'show' is the origination of that deformed megalomaniac that currently squats upon the German throne. His military ambitions will cause a war, and unfortunately the man believes that he will win it. Furthermore, there is no one in Germany, able to stop his insane ideas."

"So you truly believe a conflict may occur?" interrupted Holmes. The First Lord nodded.

"And, I can predict exactly when, Mr. Holmes," he stated.

"Germany requires a battle fleet to equal that of this country. It will take them several years to accomplish this effort, say, early in 1914.

"However, they also require a large naval port with access to the North Sea.

"I am reliably informed that the projected expansion of the port of Kiel is scheduled for completion by 1914. Add the sums together my dear fellow.

"I predict that both Germany and England will be at war by September of that year."

"What are our chances against a newly constructed German battle fleet?" said Holmes.

"Better than good," replied the First Lord. "Worse than good, should we allow the items stolen from the Dreadnaught to arrive in Germany."

"Then we shall take steps to ensure that this event never occurs, M'lord," murmured Holmes.

"Damn right!" exploded Fisher. "We'll stop the buggers dead in their tracks." Spencer Ewart and looked hard at Holmes.

"If there is anything that the Royal Navy might do to assist, it will be my duty and privilege to effect the same," he stated.

"There may well be something," said Holmes.

"Name it!" demanded the first Sea Lord.

"In the event that our proposed land assault upon the farmhouse fails and these vile specimens manage to transport the stolen equipment to the vessel in which they intend to facilitate their escape," continued Holmes. "I would be more than comforted to know that one of our warships, capable of their apprehension, might be available for this purpose."

"My God!" exploded the First Sea Lord. "You shall

have it, sir! I'll order a destroyer from the flotilla that I have at present berthed in Harwich to intercept the other vessel."

Jackie Fisher became entirely enthused with his own words.

"Damn it!" he bellowed. "I've a mind to be upon the ship myself. I crave action and have been consigned to sitting on my bottom since I commanded the landing party in that Anglo-Egyptian fiasco in '92. If you're offering the chance of action, I'm your man."

"But you are the First Sea Lord," interrupted Spencer Ewart, weakly.

"Exactly!" hooted Fisher, "and that is precisely why I am able to do it."

"There may well be considerable danger, My Lord," interjected Holmes.

"Been faced with danger all my life," commented Fisher. "Got to love it.

"Now tell me exactly how you propose to meet and settle accounts with these villains and where precisely you would wish my destroyer to be, if needed?"

Chapter Five

Piggotts Farm. North East of Lavenham, Suffolk, October, 1906

A large board proclaimed that the property was for sale. Moran couldn't believe his luck.

Upon investigating the premises, he found the principal building deserted and had moved both his men and the wagon into the same.

Upon the dawn, he had cautiously walked into Lavenham and purchased a variety of vegetables and a stewing pot. His men needed little encouragement and within a couple of hours, were feasting upon a delicious vegetable stew.

The farmhouse was not large, yet allowed Moran to retire to a small room separate from the others.

Apart from their incessant chatter, he had time to deliberate. He recalled his last meeting with von Schiffert.

The general had arrived without notice at Moran's house. He carried a canvas satchel which he placed upon the floor before taking a seat.

"All is ready?" he enquired.

"Yes," replied Moran. "My men are fully trained, and I await only the time and date from you."

"Good!" replied the other. "It has been decided that another should accompany you upon this mission. By all accounts, he is a scientific specialist who will know exactly which items to remove from the British ship. Your job is to ensure his safety throughout the entire operation and further, his safe return to Germany.

"I hate amateurs," replied Moran.

"Nevertheless," continued the other, "These are your instructions."

"And what, should our efforts not succeed?" enquired Moran. "In all operations there is a degree of failure?"

Von Schiffert moved the canvas satchel to Moran.

"Within this bag are two *StahlHandGrenaten* ," he said. "They are bombs that if ignited, are designed to utterly destroy any life forms within a 20 meter radius.

Should you decide that the mission will not succeed, you are to destroy all evidence of any that were involved upon it."

"Including your new recruit?"

"He also."

"And what of me?"

"If no evidence remains to implicate either the Kaiser or the German government of this action, your current services may be used again in another time," replied von Schiffert,

Now, as he sat upon the floor of the adjoining room within the deserted farmhouse, Moran decided that whatever the outcome, Germany might not be his best next port of call, even if the mission succeeded.

Military Headquarters, Whitehall, London, October, 1906

The First Sea Lord evidenced a state of high agitation.

"For God's sake man! An entire day has passed since our last meet. I need to know what is happening! Can't keep one of my destroyers ready for sea forever. Bad for the men's morale."

Spencer Ewart sank back defensively into his chair. "By all accounts, 'they' are in Suffolk, my Lord," he replied.

"Where in Suffolk?" demanded Fisher. "Are they anywhere near my destroyer yet?"

Holmes interrupted. "I believe that the villains that we seek, will arrive at Thorpe sometime on Saturday, M'Lord," he began. "The high tides for the following day evidence a predominance at midnight. As such, I believe that the moment for the apprehension of these miscreants will be then."

"Good!" ejaculated the First Sea Lord. "Then I can blow the swine out of the water, a little after midnight?" Holmes shook his head.

"With respect, M'Lord, it is hoped that we shall have little need of your naval assistance. The earlier assault upon the farmhouse should effectively achieve our current aims."

For a second or so, Jacky Fisher appeared aghast.

"But I need to be in on it!" he expostulated somewhat aggressively.

"Rest assured, M'Lord," replied Holmes. "We may

well have need of your valuable assistance, not in dealing with the capture of the men and the equipment at the farmhouse, but upon the event of our failure so to do, allowing the foreign vessel to escape into open water. In that instance, you alone may be the singular saviour of this country's future."

The First Sea Lord's, initially crestfallen features brightened.

"Then, I'll have my damned battle after all," he cried.

"It may appear so, M'Lord," replied Holmes quietly.

"Good!" said Fisher. "Now tell me exactly what action you propose to effect upon the beach?"

Dense Wood, North of Saxmundham, Suffolk, October, 1906

The entire operation was proceeding exactly to form. Moran couldn't believe his luck. They had been upon the road now for over seven days and apart from that unfortunate incident in the Hertfordshire wood, nothing adverse to his initial plan had occurred. What was the British government doing and more importantly, where were their operatives? Surely, some attempt to recover the items that reposed within the confines of his wagon, should have been attempted?

They would be at the coast in a day and away from England by the night of the next. It had all been too simple. Or had it?

Moran's mind strayed to his last time in Suffolk and the summer night when he and the girl had lain within his father's barn in Leiston.

For the life of him, he was unable to remember her name. She had been one of the housemaids within his father's service. Yet he recalled intensely the feeling of love and contentment, never before or ever again experienced, as her took her upon the straw.

His current thoughts were interrupted peremptorily by one of his men.

"Thought you'd like to know," said the other quietly. "There's a large hay waggon about to pass where we are."

Moran looked outside the small, wooded culvert in which his team and their own conveyance awaited the onset of the coming night.

"All of you, remain still!" he instructed.

The wagon passed creakily along the road in which Moran and his men rested and disappeared over a small rise. Moran heaved a sigh of relief.

"How much longer?" enquired Denik, one of the Dutch recruits.

"Two days at most," hissed Moran. He turned to the others.

"You have all performed exceedingly well men. Within a day or so, we shall all be safe and away from this country and in another, where your actions will afford you all, its grateful appreciation of your efforts."

"So, we have got away with it?" murmured Klaus, a German recruit.

Moran smiled broadly. "So it would appear," he said.

"Although there is the simple problem of attaining the place upon the coast, where our boat awaits."

The others began to mutter nervously amongst themselves.

Moran was up to that. "Have little fear that this action will prove successful," he began.

"We have avoided any contact with the British authorities so far, and I see little reason why the final stages of our journey to the east coast, should provide any problem." Moran actually laughed.

"From my personal experience at an early age within the county that we are presently in, I must tell you that, Suffolk inhabitants tend to be of the most parochial and private kind. More to the fact, and as a breed, they are most unwilling to involve themselves in anything outside their daily lives. I feel that, should our presence be noted by anyone, such information will remain securely locked within the breast of the voyeur." The other men appeared relieved by this statement. Moran continued.

"Today is Friday," he commented. "I plan to leave England at midnight on Sunday."

His words having apparently the desired effect, he made one last statement.

"Now, if you are all satisfied with my explanation, I think that you should attempt to get some form of rest. Tomorrow will be a long night."

Stadtscloss, Berlin, October, 1906

"Everything appears to be proceeding as planned. Herr General?" enquired the Kaiser.

"From my information, the items will be in Suffolk by tomorrow and ready for collection upon Sunday night, Your Majesty," murmured von Schiffert.

"Then, your operation appears to evidence every sign of success," said the other. Von Schiffert permitted himself a small smile of triumph.

"So it would seem, my Kaiser.

The German Emperor nodded non-committedly and stroked his moustache.

"You have done well, von Schiffert," commented the Kaiser. "But, what if your masterful plan should fail at the last moment? The British are not fools. It is too easy to believe that they will allow the theft of a piece of vital equipment to escape without some attempt to recover the same?"

"That has been taken care of, my Emperor," said von Schiffert.

"The converted gun boat to fishing vessel within which the escape is to be effected has been ordered to fire a green flare in the event that the mission has been successful. What the occupants of that craft do not know is that a high speed motor torpedo boat will accompany their voyage and stand off the coast of England, some two miles distant. Should the first craft leave without the signal, the second boat will ensure her utter destruction before she has travelled five miles seaward."

"And what if this operation achieves total success?" enquired the Kaiser.

"Then the vessel carrying the stolen equipment will be allowed to return to Kiel," replied von Schiffert. "There, the items will be transferred into safe storage and the mercenaries employed for the mission, quietly disposed of. None must remain who might indicate Your Majesty's involvement within this operation."

"I see," said the Kaiser. "And what of this Englishman Moran?" Von Schiffert shrugged his shoulders.

"His employment has always remained of limited use," he began. "His knowledge might eventually prove an embarrassment to your Majesty's position in future world affairs. I'm afraid that he will have to join his compatriots."

The German Kaiser nodded his agreement.

"So it would appear that the only two persons to be left in the world who know of this exercise are you and I, Herr General," he stated.

"So it will be, your Majesty," replied von Schiffert, without realising that his words had condemned himself. "And you may rest assured that my mouth will be stilled forever."

The German Kaiser turned away and moved over to stare again at the large picture window. Von Schiffert thus missed the softly spoken words of his Emperor.

"Of that fact, my dear general, you may certainly rest assured," he murmured.

Headquarters Military Intelligence, Whitehall, London,
October 1906

"I leave for Aldeburgh tomorrow," stated Holmes. Although I believe that those villains intend to quit our shores at midnight, two days hence, it will give me time to brief the soldiers you are supplying upon their deployment."

Spencer Ewart appeared positively miffed.

"Your assistance to date had proved most valuable, Holmes," he began. "Yet the matter in question must perforce become an army situation now."

Holmes pursed his lips. "With the greatest respect, my dear fellow, the successful outcome of this situation depends not upon brute force but, accurate intelligence, which I alone am able to supply."

Ewart sank back limply within his chair. "What exactly do you require?" he asked weakly.

"I shall require both your selected troops and their commanding officer to be in the vicinity of Aldeburgh, no later than Saturday night," said Holmes.

"I shall reserve rooms at a local hotel upon my visit tomorrow and report back to you with my final findings.

Have you decided where your men will be stationed?"

Spencer Ewart nodded. "I have discovered the presence of a retired brigadier by the name of, Hampton Morgan who occupies a country house on a large estate, some half a mile from the road between Aldeburgh and Thorpe," he announced.

"According to my sources, the old gentleman is over

the moon at being selected for an operation of which he knows little and readily agreed to the secrecy required and more to the point, insisted upon."

"Good!" replied Holmes. "Then it is time that we were away."

"Just a moment, Holmes," said Spencer Ewart.

"Whereas I concede that your investigations of the area concerned must allow you the sole privilege of instructing the commanding officer and his men as to the layout of the farmhouse and its adjacent surroundings, you are to relinquish any semblance of command, upon the commencement of military action. Is that clearly understood?"

Holmes nodded and indicated to me that we should leave.

I knew that my colleague appreciated to be able to deliver the last word in any conversation yet, was wholly unprepared when upon reaching the door, he winked at me in a most mischievous manner and looked back at Spencer Ewart.

"I trust that you enjoyed the boiled eggs for breakfast?" he enquired innocently.

The other looked puzzled. "Boiled eggs?" said he. "What the devil are you getting at, Holmes?"

"I notice to my chagrin that your normal sartorial elegance has been somewhat marred by a small yellow stain upon the left lapel of your otherwise immaculate uniform," began Holmes. Spencer Ewart began furiously scratching at the offending mark and Holmes continued.

"I am therefore able to deduce that the existing blemish was occasioned by the rather impetuous consumption of an egg or eggs at this morning's hurried breakfast. The type of stain, leads me to believe that you like your eggs of the 4-minute, viscous quality for, a further minute within the boiling water would have produced a consumable yolk of a far more congealed state and unable to find a purchase upon the spot where the other did."

I am unable to print the expletives that followed us as we quickly quit the room

Farmhouse, Between Thorpe and Aldeburgh, October, 1906

The roast chicken, though slightly overcooked, was delicious. It was the first hot meal that he had consumed over the preceding 13 days. The meal had been the provision by one of his men during the previous night's journey to Thorpe. It was highly unlikely that the Snape chicken farmer would miss the loss of three of his brood.

Moran's nasal senses had been assailed by an overriding smell upon his initial entry into the farmhouse earlier that day and enquiring upon the source of this odour, had been informed by one of the men left to guard the building, that the source emanated from an uncovered cesspit that led from a single latrine, situated some two yards from the building's back door and, continued some fifty yards to the south.

Viewing the scene outside, Moran suddenly realised that the uncovered sewer would provide a perfect means of escape if required.

Having completed his meal and his senses by now somewhat inured to the prevailing stench, Moran pushed back his chair and stood up and addressed his assembled men.

"Gentlemen," he began, "you have all done exceedingly well. Tonight, we shall all leave this country forever. However, I require a few hours of rest. I suggest that you all do the same."

Picking up the canvas satchel which he had carried since he had arrived with his team into Britain, he made his way to the stairs to the upper floor and mounted them.

Chapter Six

Googerat Barracks, Colchester, October, 1906.

Corporal William Parry's father had spent little time with his family.

At 17 William had enlisted within the army and had served in the South African war. Initially, having little grievance against the Boer farmers against whom he was sent, his senses and future commitment were occasioned when his best friend's head was shattered by the accurate bullet of a Boer sharpshooter. William, whose previous performances upon the rifle ranges at his assigned depot had been considered as somewhat below average, suddenly improved his accuracy. By the time the war concluded, William had become the master marksman within the entire regiment.

His ability had been noted by his senior officers and shortly following his return to England, he had been promoted to corporal and both offered and accepted a transfer into a "special" squad of men, valued for their proficiency within the armed services, facing a far different type of future war, than had been fought in the nineteenth century.

Equipped with the newly introduced, Lee Enfield rifle, fitted with a 4-power telescopic sight. William Parry became a most dangerous opponent to any possible adversary.

In the later stages of the 19th century, disaffected individuals seeking only the complete destruction of the accepted law and order within the countries in which they lived had formed themselves into groups, best described as anarchists. Having little thought for the chaos they might cause by their overt actions, their only commitment was the destruction of a society in which they, by their intentions, might never be included. Their savage retributions within the other states of Europe had provoked concern that a similar situation might prevail within Great Britain.

It had therefore been decided and agreed at the highest level to create and train a small team of regular soldiers that, should the worst occur, might be speedily employed to deal with any anarchistic incursion.

Shortly after having accepted the transfer to a new unit, William found himself upon a train bound for the Scottish highlands.

Upon his arrival at a small community, somewhere close to Dunbar, William and several others travelling upon the same train had been transported to a hastily constructed and heavily guarded camp which appeared to be situated within the middle of nowhere.

Within the 6 weeks that William and the other members of the selected group remained in Scotland, they had been extensively trained in the use of a variety of modern weapons and the ability to kill or maim an adversary without them. The art of stealth and concealment, including a novel idea of utilising the surrounding flora to assist this fact and known as camouflage, had been taught by a rather jolly sergeant by the name of, Mclintoch who rounded up his final address to the assembled men with the adage, "Well, ladies, I've taught ye all what I know. Keep yer bums and heads down and yer might survive. Lift either, and ye'll be dead. Good luck to ye all."

At the completion of the course and from an initial intake of some 100 soldiers, only 50 had been selected for further use. The remainder being returned to their respective regiments.

William was one of those who remained. He was relieved that another soldier, Jack Morris had also proved acceptable to those responsible for the final selection.

Within the earlier 6 weeks of intensive training, Jack had become a close friend.

Upon their private conversations, William learned the fact that both his and Jack's antecedents were of little difference.

Jack had been born in Suffolk where his father, serving in India, enjoyed a senior military rank. Jack never knew his father.

His parental recollections appeared somewhat hazy. Due to the death of his mother following his sixth birthday, shortly followed by what he knew, his father had mysteriously left his regiment and returned to England. To date, Jack's father had never attempted to make any contact with his son but arranged that, Jack be deposited into the care of an aged aunt until he was of sufficient age, whereupon he had been sent to a Methodist boarding school in Bury, St. Edmunds, and remained there within the harsh conditions of that time, until his fifteenth birthday, when he enlisted in the British army.

The rigorous and unrelenting dictates of his boarding school had hardened the boy to similar conditions within the army of the time and the companionship and feeling of belonging to a companionship that he had never before experienced, conditioned a love for his new life.

It was early in his service life that Jack discovered the real name of his absent parent and from thereon, refused to be drawn upon the subject.

He would defer any investigation upon this aspect, with the remark, "My father's name is forever blemished by what I have discovered to be the most spurious and degrading actions upon his part. It shall remain a secret and I would respect any to allow it so to be."

Following their period of intensive training, the selected men were transferred to specially constructed barracks in Colchester, Essex. To avoid any unnecessary publicity, the new company, officially to be known as company "T" had been designated a special section within the British army, formed to deal with acts of minor insurgence within the realm.

Colchester, by its easy rail access to most parts of the

country, was thus deemed to be an ideal for the new company's headquarters.

However, their strict training for action began to clash with the lengthening period of their relative period of ease and misuse as they awaited their summons for the duty they required.

Officer's Quarters, Googerat Barracks, Colchester, October, 1906

Anthony Fyfe-Smythe had been born the second son of Lord Grenfell and as such, inherited the privileges associated within the position of his birth.

From an early age, he had decided that the elitishness evidenced by his peers and false appreciation bestowed upon the so-called upper classes by those of lesser standing within the structure of the day, was a situation that bore little valuable merit and wished to have none of it.

Thus, at the age of 17 years, he quit the family home and joined the British army as a common private. HIs father, learning of the wayward antic of his second son, immediately disinherited the lad from any participation that he might have enjoyed within the considerable wealth upon the baron's death. Being advised of this fact, did little to deter the lad's determination to make a name for himself outside the society that would have normally protected any action upon his part.

Anthony's ability and nerve within his actions during

both the re-conquest of the Sudan and further, the South African war against the Boers, gained him the unreserved respect of the soldiers who served with him. In, 1902, he was gazetted second lieutenant and unbelievably, for promotions at that time were slow, awarded his captaincy in, March, 1904.

His mercurial career had been carefully watched by Spencer Ewart and thus in early 1906 and upon the persuasive arguments offered by that respected individual to his superiors, he had been appointed to command "T" company.

Arriving in Colchester in February, he had realised the lustreless condition of the men and immediately set about a period of intensive training.

By the end of July, he had earned the love, hatred and eternal respect of all those under his command. The men loved him because he was a "ranker" and one of them. They hated him for his harsh impositions and acceptance of only 100 per cent effort upon their part and, they respected him, for they knew that his reasoned logic and his care for the life of his soldiers, would protect them from the, ignorant, unqualified, outrageous and lethal decisions of more senior officers that had caused the bloody slaughter of their mates within the recent South African campaigns.

By, late August, Company "T" were ready for deployment, and as nothing foreseeable appeared to be active upon the horizon to which they had been trained, Anthony Fyfe-Smythe gave them a month's leave.

Shortly following their return to barracks, the company was informed that a situation had arisen where their special talents would be required.

Neo-Georgian building, North-East of Aldeburgh, October, 1906

Glenton House squatted dominantly upon the 3 acres of land in which it sat.

Brigadier Hampton Morgan had discovered its existence shortly following his retirement from a lifetime of service to his country, immediately fallen in love with the site and purchased it with the funds bequeathed to his wife from her late father's will.

The brigadier found the place delightful and more to the fact private.

The only blight upon the entire estate was the presence of a small yet obtrusive building that sat within the far corner of the grounds.

The previous owner, himself a retired army colonel, had constructed the building as a school house for the orphaned children of serving soldiers, killed in the action to recover the Sudan, in which he figured.

Few soldiers from Aldeburgh had died in this action and thus, the school was somewhat leanly attended. Nevertheless, for the odd child, it had provided an educational opportunity unavailable elsewhere.

Whereas the present incumbent wished the structure to be immediately dismantled, his charming wife, insisted upon the preservation of the schoolhouse. His wife's latent fortune ensured her success in any dispute affecting the small premises.

His continued depreciation of the small structure was greatly mollified, upon receiving an instruction from the highest level, that his hated edifice was required to form part of a highly secret operation of which he neither had a part nor might enquire further upon.

"What could I say to that?" he grumbled happily.

Aldeburgh, Suffolk, October, 1906

We had arrived early that Friday morning.

Holmes insisted that we obtain rooms at the Brudenell Hotel which, apart from its location to the beach, provided the most excellent dining menu.

Holmes registered ourselves as Somes and Crayston, stating that we were ecologists inspecting the seashore and would require our rooms for the nights of the coming Saturday and Sunday only.

"I do not believe that the poor desk clerk had any idea of what an ecologist is," remarked Holmes.

Having had nothing to eat following my early rousing, my salivary gland had tweaked agonisingly upon my study of the hotel's breakfast offerings and having suggested that we avail ourselves of the fare, I was more than aggrieved by my friend's outburst that, "We should not consider trivialities at such a time." Without more ado, we left the hotel.

Holmes had insisted that we both "dress down" into clothes more befitting our assumed profession.

"A frock coat, starched collar and child's fishing net, would hardly be associated as correct by an observant viewer," he stated.

He also insisted that our proposed passage between Aldeburgh and Thorpe be made upon the foreshore that connected the two communities.

"The height of the road and the slope of the beach, will allow us to remain unseen by anyone at the farmhouse," he said.

Thus we trudged through the sand and shingle for at least a quarter of a mile to the section of the shore where the jetty prodded the cold waters of the North Sea.

I am a fair pedestrian upon the solid, granite slabs of London but the forgiving particles of the sandy beach began to affect my legs to an extent that by the time we reached the stained, wooden uprights of the timber landing platform, I required a rest from my exertions.

I sat down upon the beach and took out a cigarette.

Meanwhile Holmes wandered around the foreshore, apparently intent on studying the lapping tide. Finally he returned to where I sat.

"Just as I thought!" he muttered to no one in particular. "It's a perfect spot."

"To what are you referring, Holmes?" said I.

"The disposition of sand, my dear fellow," replied Holmes.

"What of it?" I countered.

"The morning tide is receding," stated Holmes. "Thus, it allows me to clearly view the extent of the high water mark. Whereas upon the remainder of the beach to Thorpe the sand slopes gently into the sea providing little depth for even a vessel of the shallowest draught, it is at this precise point that the coast shelves deeply, permitting a craft of more robust construction to safely moor up at this jetty."

Holmes smacked his hand against one of the timber uprights.

"My God Watson!" he cried. "The individual who planned this deed is a veritable master of detail. In normal circumstances, I would willingly shake his hand."

"And, if it is Moran?" said I.

Holmes looked at me coldly. "Outright stupidity does not sit well upon you, my dear friend," he replied.

"Come!" he continued. "We have yet to survey the farmhouse."

I rose from my position and we both made our way to the spot where the beach encountered the road.

Military Headquarters, Whitehall, London, October 1906

"Well! Any news?" roared the First Sea Lord.

"None as such M'lord" replied Spencer Ewart. "Holmes is due back later this day with his final observations. I will inform you of any further news as soon as I receive the same."

Jackie Fisher snorted. "Can't keep a destroyer under orders waiting around too long," he bleated rather lamely. "Ain't good for the discipline of the service."

The First Lord paused, leant over the other's desk and fixed his eyes upon Spencer Ewart.

"What's that on your lapel," he enquired. "Looks like an egg stain to me."

Evart's face turned crimson. "Stain? I never realised it was there, M'lord," he stammered.

"Well, whatever the damn thing is," thundered Jackie Fisher, "be good enough to have the mark removed. Ain't good for senior officers to appear un-dressed."

With that comment, Fisher trundled out of the room.

For a second or so, Spencer Ewart sat rigidly upon his chair then slamming his right hand firmly down upon his highly polished, leather-topped desk, he rose, made for the door of his office, opened it and screamed at the poor cypher clerk that sat in a small desk in the outer office.

"Castairs! Get my damned batman!"

Aldeburgh, Suffolk, October 1906

We had arrived to a portion of the beach where it joined the road. Luckily, the final two to three yards enjoyed the heavy infestation of long sea grass that permitted us to survey the land leading from the other side of the road to the farmhouse in relative secrecy.

For a few minutes. Holmes studied the land through his powerful field glasses.

"You will note that the original timber cladding that encased the low building to the right of the farmhouse has been removed since our last visit." he murmured. I obviously looked blank. Holmes smiled and shook his head.

"Dear Watson," he said softly. "At times, so

unobservant yet at all times, so utterly valuable."

"What of this building?" I enquired.

"Its original purpose was that of a smoke house," replied Holmes patiently.

"As such and to be effective, it required total and sealed encapsulation to allow for the successful fumigation of the products for which it was constructed."

"And the side wall that has now been removed?" said I.

"Obviously to allow the storage of the vehicle carrying the stolen articles from Portsmouth," answered Holmes. He handed me his field glasses.

"Look for yourself."

I peered through the lenses. The farmhouse appeared to be deserted.

"It's empty, there is no one there," I remarked.

"Don't you believe it Watson? Do you not notice that thin wisps of wood smoke coming from the far chimney? The building is occupied."

"But there is no sign of the cart."

"That will arrive with the main party overnight. Of that I am certain," said Holmes.

"We shall remain in our hotel this evening and early tomorrow I will make a quick inspection of the place again.

"If my deductions are correct, I shall contact Colchester and arrange for the soldiers to be here early tomorrow night for their final briefing."

Chapter Seven

HMS Dauntless, Harwich, October, 1906

The first officer was impatient.

"What is your problem, Wilson?" he enquired of his subordinate.

"There is a funny looking, little chap, wearing sea boots and a jumper demanding to come aboard, sir," he answered.

"Well, get rid of him," ordered the first officer, irritably.

"That's just the problem, sir," said the other. "He won't go away."

The first officer shuddered. "Very well, I'll deal with him," he said angrily.

Making his way to the lower deck, he confronted the new arrival.

"Who are you?" he stated. The other's eyes bulged.

"Who am I?" his voice thundered. "Do you not know?"

"From your attire," replied the first officer, "I would assume you to be a Gypsy. Now will you leave my ship?"

The other moved to the gangplank and indicated to someone upon the dock below. Within a few moments, another man arrived on board, wearing the uniform of a Vice Admiral.

The first officer stood back and saluted.

"Tell him!" ordered the "Gypsy".

"You have aboard this ship, Sir John Fisher, First Lord

of the Admiralty," he announced. The first officer's features blanched.

"My lord, my apologies. I did not know," he began. Fisher waved his explanations aside.

"Don't need your apologies," he replied. "Good to know that my officers act as I would expect. Would never let an individual dressed as I am aboard any ship that I commanded. Think nothing of it. Now, take me to your captain!"

Aldeburgh, October 1906

Holmes and I advanced into the school room followed by Captain Fyfe-Smythe.

The assembled soldiers attempted to rise from the confines of their children's designed desks and seats but their captain signified that they should remain seated.

Holmes approached the blackboard and for a few moments, sketched the outline of the Suffolk coast, the jetty and the farmhouse upon the cleaned surface. Having completed his drawing, he stood back and addressed the assembled company.

"Gentlemen," he began. "What you see before you is the outline of the land within which you have to operate. I have intensely studied the area concerned and the drawing depicted here, is but an indication of the shoreline and the farmhouse, the object of this exercise. I will now leave it to your officer to brief you further."

With that, Holmes moved aside and Fyfe-Smythe took the stage.

"Initially, I would like to thank both Mr. Holmes and Doctor Watson for their invaluable information upon this exercise," he began. "Rarely has an operation begun with such brilliant intelligence." He turned to Holmes and me. "Gentlemen, you have my sincere thanks."

Holmes had not completely finished.

"I believe captain, that I should advise all here upon the name and reputation of the principal we believe to be involved in the entire operation and if so, he will certainly be amongst those that we seek to apprehend this night."

"If you feel that such information is necessary, Holmes then please begin."

"His name is Moran," said Holmes. "A name quite possibly unknown to the rest of you, but be advised, the man is of the most dangerous and merciless persuasion. He will never allow himself to be easily taken."

The other members of the room were far too intent upon Holmes's final words to notice the immediate effect these produced upon the face of Jack Morris, whose features grew pale in shock.

Fyfe-Smythe picked up a tapered wooden staff and smacked the pointer upon the blackboard.

"Here is the object of our action, the farmhouse," he began. "This and his stick settled upon Holmes's sketch of the jetty, "is the point where we must ensure none of the enemy ever reaches." His pointer slid across to an area some 200 yards from the jetty and stopped.

"It is here," he continued, "that we shall site our Maxim machine gun. This in itself will be our last resort. Nothing living must leave our shores. Do I make myself completely understood?" The assembled men grunted their affirmation.

"Whereas, our object is the entire annihilation of the enemy force, any that show a positive intention to surrender, must be spared for future interrogation," continued Fyfe-Smythe. "Is that also clear to you all?" Again the men grunted.

"Good! Now to the operation itself," the captain returned to the blackboard.

"You will note that the farmhouse, which is our principal objective, is surrounded by a brick wall, which apart from encapsulating the men we seek to destroy within the building, will also provide a perfect firing pit for three marksmen. You will also note that the land adjacent to the farmhouse is bisected by several drainage dykes and these must be avoided at all cost to allow effective deployment of our existing forces.

It is estimated that our present opposition consists of no more than twelve enemy agents and that in itself would appear to present little problem, if our assault is both silent and unexpected." He turned to a man, bearing the stripes of a sergeant.

"Sergeant Wilkins!" The other attempted to rise from his children's desk. Fyfe-Smythe indicated that he remain seated.

"Put three of you best marksmen behind the wall at the front of the farmhouse," he ordered.

"As you say, sir. It will be done," replied the other.

"Who are you placing upon the Maxim?" asked the captain.

"Corporal Parry to operate the weapon and Private Morris as loader, sir," barked Wilkins.

"As the entire operation will be effected under the cover of darkness," continued Fyfe-Smythe, "it will be necessary to provide some illumination to the beach area and Army Ordnance has kindly supplied a carbide searchlight and two men to operate the gadget. The light will be positioned between the machine gun and the road from Aldeburgh to Thorpe and some few yards in front of the weapon and, only illuminated upon the advent of small arms fire from the farmhouse.

As far as that building is concerned, I expect some internal lighting will be evidenced to assist the men assigned to the brick wall to discover targets if the need arises. If for any reason, the farmhouse is in darkness, each sharpshooter at the wall will be provided with a powerful flashlight which, will be switched on, the moment any firearms are employed and not before. Are my instructions clearly understood?"

The assembled men mumbled their assent.

Fyfe-Smythe returned to the blackboard.

"Sergeant Wilkins and I will take up positions upon the left of the marksman at the wall. I shall have a loud hailer with which to call upon those within the farmhouse to surrender. In the event that my summons is accepted then, those that emerge from the building are to be relieved of any weapons and brought to a point here!" and he indicated an area, just outside the perimeter brick wall.

"If the occupants within the building decide to put up a fight, you are all authorised to shoot to kill."

Fyfe-Smythe sought a stick of chalk from the tray beneath the blackboard and quickly drew a series of small circles around the building. He addressed Sergeant Wilkins again.

"These are the respective dispositions of your remaining men," he announced.

"If you now look again at the blackboard, you will note a series of deep trenches or dykes that bisect the land to the west of the road. You will also note that these ditches stop short of the main town of Aldeburgh. You will also see," and he tapped the blackboard with his pointer to an area of Holmes's original drawing, bearing a large "X", followed by a series of broken arrows to a point upon the connecting road, some 50 yards from the town's northern boundary, "that the route we will follow, allows us relative secrecy from our present situation to an area where our final assault may begin..

Those designated to form the encircling section of our squad may deploy to the rear of the farmhouse here, without fear of encountering any existing dykes. The remainder will move to the beach where the slope to the road will conceal our presence from any in the farmhouse."

Fyfe-Smythe looked at his wristwatch.

"It is now 21 hundred," he stated. We move out to take up our positions at 21.45.
"We shall be in our assigned positions by, 22.30 hrs. Allowing additional time for the men surrounding the farmhouse, we shall be both ready and able to commence our attack by, 2300." He paused. "You all know your positions and what is required of you. It only remains for me to wish you the best of luck."

The other men extricated themselves from their seats, stood up and began to mingle. Fyfe-Smythe came over to where Holmes and I stood. At the time. Holmes was in the action of replacing his gold Hunter within the confines of his waistcoat pocket.
"I see that you still rely upon your pocket watch." said the captain.
Holmes regarded the other soberly. "Correspondingly, I note that you rely upon a goldsmith's wristwatch," he replied.
"Excellent timepiece," stated the other. "Recommended to me by a fellow officer who served in the South African war. Never lost a minute."
Holmes sighed. "Then you have me to some advantage," he murmured. "My Hunter has lost some three seconds over the last ten years. Then again, if one accepts that the existence of this planet may be measured in thousands of millennia, what is but three

small moments?"

Holmes finally seated his timepiece.

"Now!" he enquired. "Where do you wish both Watson and I to be stationed in the coming attack?"

Fyfe-Smythe appeared aghast. "But you cannot be any part of the proposed action," he stammered. "Civilians within a military operation are most definitely not on. Oh no! Your presence must most decidedly be far away from any possible source of danger!"

I could sense the hackles upon my colleague's neck. He glowered at the captain and his next words bore an icy frost. "My dear chap," he began. "Both Watson and I have been in many situations where the presence of imminent danger would be considered far worse than the present action. It is upon my own investigations and deductions that we are here tonight. I insist that we are present upon the final completion of this matter."

The other appeared totally nonplussed by this. "I shall require confirmation of your acceptability from higher sources," he stammered.

"There is no time for that!" stated Holmes.

"Then, perhaps some written disclaimer, in the event that either of you are wounded or worse," began Fyfe-Smythe. The ice upon Holmes's next words pervaded the room.

"I am not given to append my signature to any such document," he growled.

"Paper has the infernal habit of being either destroyed, lost or intentionally mislaid."

He glowered at the other.

"My word is my bond," he hissed. "Those who know

me well, accept this.

"Should any ill befall either myself or Doctor Watson, you have my assurance that no action or claim upon our part will result. Will that be sufficient?"

Fyfe-Smythe realised that he had lost and shrugged hopelessly.

"Very well, Mr. Holmes, you may accompany us but, stay close to me at all times."

At that point, the captain turned to speak with Sergeant Wilkins and thus missed Holmes's muttered words to me.

"Staying close to that individual," he murmured somewhat ruefully, "may have placed the both of us in greater danger than had we walked into that farmhouse, introduced ourselves to those villains and politely required them to surrender."

Stadtschloss, Berlin, October 1906

The Kaiserin was concerned. The Crown Prince had developed a high temperature.

"You must attend this reception on your own," she stated.

"The boy has a cold, that is all," said the Kaiser. "For goodness sake woman, finish your dressing. We are due at this damned pantomime in half an hour and you know how the British will relish any tardiness upon our part?"

His sharpness upset his wife. Her eyes filled with tears.

Noticing this, the Kaiser crossed the room and gathered his wife into his arms. His tone softened.

"Please forgive my behaviour, my dearest," he murmured. I have pressing political matters upon my mind."

Immediately, his wife shook herself from her condition. "Darling Willy, please forgive me for forgetting to understand the troubles of a great Emperor. Of course I shall attend with you tonight." She kissed him hard.

Tonight, we shall show those stupid British the true potential of the new German empire." The Kaiserin hurried away to complete her wardrobe.

The Kaiser, left upon his own, with his wife's departing words ringing in his ears, raised his eyes and silently murmured, "God willing, we shall!"

Aldeburgh, Suffolk, October. 1906

We had made our way to the road bisecting the town of Aldeburgh and the village of Thorpe.

Holmes had initially resisted the black cotton costume that Fyfe-Smythe had insisted that we all wear but had been convinced that this attire would render us as shadows only within the moonlit scene.

Together with the captain and the three appointed marksmen, we gained the small perimeter wall of the farmhouse, without note, crouched low and waited.

Farmhouse, Thorpe - Aldeburgh road, Night, October 1906

The large single, ground floor room that provided the daytime accommodation, glowed with the illumination of several kerosene fuelled lanterns. A profusion of candles, installed by the present incumbents, flickered in their containers and added a degree of further brightness to the otherwise sombre surroundings.
The assembled men sat mainly quiet within their own thoughts.

The main door opened and the burly Dutchman entered.

"Nothing happening out there," he stated. "Who's standing guard next?
One of the Belgians groaned and began to rise from his seat upon the floor.
"My turn," he muttered, picking up his rifle and moving to the door. "What time do we expect the boat?"
"Around midnight," answered a man from Dusseldorf
"Good!" replied the other. "I've only got about a half an hour outside and the temperature is getting chilly."

Karl Stollig got up from the small chair in which he had been sitting. He was dreadfully afraid and never dreamed in his wildest nightmares of being involved within the current situation he now found himself. He was a scientist not a murderer. He needed to escape but

175

how? He needed to think away from the presence of the others - but where? His bladder provided the answer.

"Where are you going, lad?" said the man from Dusseldorf.
"I need to pass water," stammered Karl.
"Well, go on and do it," replied the other. "And don't be long about it!"
Karl left the room and moved outside.
"Don't like that one," grumbled the Dutchman. "Not really one of us."

Reaching the door to the *privy*, he moved to the juncture in the broken wall and looked out upon the scene.
The bright October moon had transformed the green grass that surrounded the farmhouse into a silvery-grey carpet, bisected by dark shadows.
To his left, a shadow moved. Of that Karl was most certain. Then, to his right, two more. Yes, they really did. It wasn't his imagination.
Karl panicked. His previous distress about the situation that he had become recently and unwittingly involved in turned to pure terror.

His adrenal gland, pumped hot streams of vibrant energy into his previously frozen form, alerting his primal instinct for survival and with a mighty bound through the brick aperture and an incredible leap over the midden trench. He ran away from the farmhouse. In which direction, he cared not.

His flight was brought short after some 50 paces by the smack of a rifle butt upon his head. Even the adrenalin did little to allay his immediate unconsciousness and thus he missed the grunt of his assailant.

"Where do you think you're going, mate?"

Exterior Farmhouse, Thorpe - Aldeburgh road, 2350 hrs. October 1906

Pierre Muessele grinned. From his position on sentry duty to the front of the building, he had seen the navigational lights of the vessel's approach and come to rest at the jetty.

"Merde Anglais!" he whispered to himself.

He wandered to the small wall that surrounded the farmhouse and it was precisely at that point, that his current thoughts were rudely extinguished by the barrel of a rifle that poked painfully into his sternum.

Pierre might have disliked the English but he was no fool. He immediately dropped his own weapon and accepted the rough hands that hauled his body over the wall and bound his wrists securely.

Captain Fyfe-Smythe raised his loud hailer and bellowed into the mouth piece.

"This is the British army! You are completely surrounded! Discard your weapons and come out with your hands up and your lives will be spared."

Interior Farmhouse, Thorpe - Aldeburgh road, 2351 hrs. October 1906

None of the men fully understood English, and the distortion of the voice from outside made even simple comprehension difficult.

All they understood was that their recent position had been threatened by another and as one, they scrambled for their weapons, smashed the glass in the windows and began to give fire into the darkness.

Upstairs, Moran realised that the game was up. His mission had failed. Now, he needed to escape the present situation.

Removing the two *StahlHandGrenaten* from the satchel, he left his room, descended the stairs, primed the bombs and tossed them into the main room of the farmhouse, then quickly made his way to the door to the outside privy.

The remaining men of his earlier team never heard the twin detonations that blew them to smithereens.

Exterior Farmhouse, Thorpe - Aldeburgh road, 2352 hrs. October 1906

"Open fire!" commanded Fyfe-Smythe.

The riflemen at the wall were all professionals. Since the mistakes of the South African war, the British army had been rigorously trained to fire 10 aimed shots a minute.

In their haste to repel any outsiders, the men within the farmhouse had failed to extinguish the internal illumination of the building and thus their individual forms stood out as clearly defined targets against the light.

One by one, they collapsed beneath the accurate fire of the soldiers.

Brick wall, front of Farmhouse, October 1906

Holmes and I had been ordered to stay within the protection of the wall.
I could sense my colleague's frustration in finding himself unable to see exactly what was occurring. Fyfe-Smythe crouched with us, occasionally rising to peer over the wall yet at the same time, signalling to us to keep down.
Suddenly, the muffled reports of two explosions split the night air and the lower, front windows of the building erupted in gouts of flame and debris.
Fyfe-Smythe was on his feet in an instant. I noted that his physical stature slumped visibly. For a few moments he stared at the smoking building then, spoke quietly to his riflemen.
"Cease firing!" he commanded wearily.

Open land surrounding the Farmhouse, October, 1906

Moran made his way cautiously through the clumps of stagnant reed.

He could distinguish the road and the beach and the occasional glare from the muzzles of several rifles and the continuous flash from a machine gun.

From his present position, he would be obliged to pass along a stretch of sand between the automatic weapon and the sea. This in itself should present little problem since, the glare of the forward sighted searchlight, allowed little visual perception of anything or anybody behind the point of its installation. Avoiding the machine gun, Moran made his way around the weapon. Suddenly, his right foot was filled with cold sea water. He cursed silently. He had forgotten the incoming high tide. Now, any further means of escape would mean direct contact with the men manning the weapon.

Moving quickly towards the machine gunner and his mate and finding that the same were clearly outlined against the searchlight's beam, Moran shot them both. He knew he had hit the machine gunner for the man toppled over by his weapon. The other he was unsure of since the figure appeared to roll away as Moran fired. It mattered not, he was clear to make his escape to the waiting boat.

As he ran across the unforgiving sand to where the craft of his imminent salvation waited, he realised that his figure was illuminated but cared little.

Holmes and Fyfe-Smythe reached the end of the path leading from the burning farmhouse and halted.

"Am I required, sir?" enquired a disembodied voice within the darkness that surrounded them. It was Charlie Dell, one of the sharpshooters who had accompanied us to the wall of the farmhouse.

"I think not, corporal." replied Fyfe-Smythe. "The entire matter appears to have been most satisfactorily concluded."

"The German boat seems to be leaving," announced Holmes. "The First Sea Lord can deal with that matter." Holmes raised his binoculars and regarded the scene at the shore, then he stiffened.

"Good God!" he cried, "There's someone making for the boat!"

Holmes raised his glasses again.

"It's Moran!" he yelled.

"Take him out!" ordered Fyfe-Smythe. Dell demurred.

"Don't like moving targets with this ruddy scope," he grunted. "At this range, prefer open sights."

With that remark Dell unclipped the cumbersome sniper scope from his Lee Enfield, raised the weapon, took aim and applied "first" pressure to the trigger.

Suffolk beach, October, 1906

Moran knew that he would be safe. It was only some thirty yards to the jetty. He had made it. He could make out the hurried preparations for the vessel's departure but these would not interfere with his assured arrival, before it finally left its berth.

In his haste to be away from the possible slaughter of the machine gunner and his mate, he had failed to notice that the latter had risen to his feet and was actively pursuing his own progress along the beach.

The night was calm yet, a brisk breeze swirled along the foreshore, totally obliterating normal conversation thus, he failed to hear the repeated outcries of his pursuer.

It was only upon reaching the jetty that he both halted and realised that he had been followed. Having discarded his pistol during his flight along the beach. Moran turned aggressively to receive the oncoming figure.

"Dad! It's me!" cried the youth who then that threw itself into Moran's unsuspecting embrace.

Aldeburgh - Thorpe road, October, 1906

"Take the shot!" ordered Fyfe-Smythe.

Dell squeezed the trigger.

The Short Magazine Lee Enfield fired a round that travelled at a speed of, 2490 feet per second. It took precisely 2/10's of a second to reach Moran which was exactly the time it needed for Jack Morris to reach his father.

The .303 dum-dum round smashed into Jack's yielding flesh, expanded and mashed into pulp his upper chest organs. Moran's luck held. If a normal bullet had been used, it would possibly have passed through the body of the young soldier and into his own.

For a second, Moran stared down into the anguished, floodlit features of the lad and heard the dying words of the young soldier.

"Dad...oh dad, it hurts..." murmured the youth. Then the eyes closed and the body fell from his arms onto the soft, damp sand.

Then self-preservation took control of his senses and leaving the dead soldier, Moran made for the jetty.

Easily making the platform, he saw that the vessel assigned for their rescue was making off and had already reached the end of the pier. Tearing along the jetty he took a mighty leap and fell in a huddled heap upon the after deck.

He was safe. Damn the others.

Aldeburgh - Thorpe road, October, 1906

I had managed to catch up with Holmes and the captain and was therefore present when Dell took his shot.

"I don't believe it!" cried Holmes. "The villain's got away." He turned to me.

"Watson," he commanded, "use your flare!"

I fumbled within the satchel that I had been carrying and found the object. It was only a long tube with a string poking from one end. Offering the stringed end

183

to the night sky, I pulled the ignition cord. The effect was most impressive.

With a shudder, no more of a jolt, an incandescent ball of red light whooshed from my right hand and arced up, illuminating the dark sky.

Holmes and the captain watched its progress.

"Well, it's up to the First Lord and his destroyer now," commented Holmes drily.

HMS Dauntless, Off the Suffolk Coast, North Sea, October, 1906

Aboard His Majesty's destroyer, Dauntless, the First Sea Lord stamped his rubber clad feet against the impending autumn chill.

The vessel lay some mile or so from the hamlet of Thorpe and several hundred yards from the coast. With her steam turbines hot yet stilled from any required power, no sound filled the calm night other than the quietly spoken commands of her captain.

Fisher was worried. It was past midnight yet, as he peered through his binoculars, he could determine little activity within the section of the coast, selected by Holmes to be the eventual embarcation point of the villains and their gain.

"What the hell's happening?" he muttered, turning to the warship's commander who stood beside him upon the bridge.

"Give them time, M'Lord," answered Lieutenant Austin Hargreaves. "It is only just past the hour."

Suddenly, the muted sounds of gunfire broke the stillness of the quiet night and the bright beam of a land-based searchlight flooded the coastal area in question.

"Where's that damn flare?" muttered the First Sea Lord.

As if in answer to his question, a bright streak of red screamed into the dark sky.

"Ah! That's more like it," grunted the First Sea Lord. "Now, we have some action." He looked again at Hargreaves. "Start engines, full ahead, lieutenant!"

"Aye, aye, M'Lord!" replied Hargreaves. "Start engines, full ahead, number one!"

Suddenly the entire vessel shuddered with the massive power of her steam turbines.

Lieutenant Hargreaves cast a glance at his helmsman.

"Bring her over to port!" he ordered.

The First Sea Lord was far too interested in the possibility of the coming action to notice the visual response from the helmsman to his captain.

The raised eyebrows and mouthed words, "Bloody admirals" was thus lost to recorded naval history.

Fisher was up for action.

"I see them, Hargreaves. My God she's moving. She's getting away!" he bellowed.

"Switch on our own searchlight!"

For a second nothing happened then, with a burst of brilliance, the entire sea area became starkly illuminated by the destroyer's powerful light beam.

"There she is!" cried Fisher. "Now we have her!"

He turned again to Hargreaves.

"Order a shot over her bow," be began, then halted. "No! Damn it! Sink her!"

For a moment the First Sea Lord became as a youth with his first real toy.

"Might I give the order, Lieutenant," he queried boyishly. "It will be my last chance of real action." Hargreaves nodded and grinned his acceptance.

"Which tube is it?" said Fisher. Hargreaves indicated the item concerned.

In his excitement, Fisher actually lunged over and grabbed the voice-pipe.

"This is the First Sea Lord," he roared. "Fire for effect at the vessel at," he looked up at Hargreaves for confirmation. "Red 2.0" replied the other. Fisher returned to the pipe. "Red 2.0." he commanded.

"Oh yes! And I'm the King of England," came the tinny response.

Unnoticed in the dark, Fisher's features became infused with outrage.

Lieutenant Hargreaves was about to step in then Fisher calmed himself.

"I am the First Sea Lord," he began. "Should you wish your captain to confirm this fact to you, he is here beside me."

The other voice replied.

"Your order is confirmed, M'lord. Guns will open fire immediately."

At that, and with a bright flash and tremendous report, the 12-pounder main armament opened up.

Fisher watched the fall of shot. He returned to the voice

pipe.

"30 yards in front," he said.

Within a few seconds the 12-pounder cracked again.

"On target but 20 yards short," commented Fisher. "There's a fiver for you if you hit the bastard on the next shot."

The tinny voice cheekily replied.

"If there's real money on it, watch this, M'lord."

A further few seconds elapsed before the 12-pounder cracked loudly again.

As Fisher watched, the other craft suddenly erupted in an incandescent ball of fire and debris. All that remained was a flame-soaked hull that slowly sank into the dark waters of the North Sea.

Fisher relaxed and addressed Hargreaves.

"Make to Admiralty: Mission accomplished: Am returning to port."

"Shall I send in code?" enquired Hargreaves. The First Sea Lord shook his head adamantly.

"No! Let any of the foreign bastards know that may be listening in, that their vile attempt has failed," he stated.

German Motor Torpedo boat, North Sea, October, 1906

Two miles out, the high speed German torpedo boat *Komet*, her powerful engines silenced, wallowed in the gentle swell of the ocean.

Upon her small bridge, *Leutenant-zur-See* Kristian Dietmcycr had witnessed the destruction of the other craft. Sighing audibly, he turned to his first officer.

"Make to General von Schiffert, German Military Headquarters, Zossen, Berlin," he began. "Message reads, 'Delivery of package failed; no sign of any postmen,' am returning to base." The other disappeared to carry out his instruction. Dietmeyer was left alone on the bridge with his helmsman.

Watching the final moments of the flaming vessel, he put down his Zeiss glasses and without turning to his helmsman spoke loudly enough for the other to hear.

"Not a good night for the Imperial German navy, Klause?"

"Never really liked fireworks myself, *Herr Kaleut*," replied the disembodied voice of the other.

For a brief moment, Dietmeyer permitted himself a chuckle at the wry humour of his helmsman. Then his inured sense of command re-asserted itself.

Grabbing the voice-pipe he ordered, "Start engines! Full ahead!"

His attention returned to Klause.

"Now, get us out of here before that damn British destroyer discovers us and adds another scalp to its pole. Make for Kiel!"

Chapter Eight

North Sea, off the Suffolk coast, October, 1906

Illuminated by the glare of the destroyer's searchlight, Moran clung to the gunwales of the German craft. For the first time in his life confusion had both entered and addled his active brain.

The young man, who had sacrificed his life upon the beach to protect him, had stated that he was his son. Could that be? He tried to think back, but the current situation prohibited this effort.

His current situation took priority upon the second salvo from the British vessel.

He had lost and his foreseeable future was assured unless he took immediate action. The assembled deck crew appeared unable to comprehend their current predicament.

Moran sought about and discovered a ship's lifebuoy, hanging by the forward hatch.

It took but a moment for him to detach the item from its purchase and toss the same into the dark waters of the North Sea. Pausing for a moment to curse his adversary, Moran heaved himself over the side and into the freezing water

From the shoreline, Holmes, Fyfe-Smythe and I, watched the disintegration of the enemy vessel in silence. Holmes eventually broke it.

"Well, that's the end of it." he remarked.

The two, ambulances requested by, Fyfe-Smythe had arrived upon the scene and their personnel were in the process of removing the dead and injured from both the actions at the farmhouse and the beach.

"Who the devil was that soldier who nearly wrecked the entire operation," said Holmes.

"I know not yet," replied Fyfe-Smythe. "Yet, rest assured, whoever he might be, he will shortly face a court-martial for his incautious and unseemly action that might have resulted in the destruction of the entire plan."

At this moment, two stretcher bearers passed us, carrying the body of Parry.

The wounded soldier cried out to us.

"Don't blame Morris, sir. The man you were after was his dad. He was only trying to save him. "He meant no harm."

"That will not save him," commented Fyfe-Smythe. "I am determined to press charges."

The leading stretcher bearer spoke.

"Don't seem no point, sir. That lad on the beach is as dead as mutton."

Fyfe-Smythe appeared confused.

Gently taking his arm and guiding him from the beach, Holmes quietly suggested, "The night has been long, yet successful. I believe that it is now time to go home.

Military Headquarters, Whitehall, London, October 1906

Spencer Ewart sat at his desk in Whitehall.

It was almost half past twelve and he had received no information from his sources.

Holmes had assiduously insisted that the previous night was the moment when the action to recover the stolen items would take place, yet he had heard nothing.

His anxiety continued for the space of a further half hour until the arrival of a telecommunications officer who handed him a piece of paper.

Spencer Ewart grabbed the document and studied its contents. The operation had been totally successful, and the cypher signed by Fisher himself.

Casting the brief message upon his desk, Spencer Ewart moved to the bureau and poured himself large Dimple Haig.

Farmhouse, Between Thorpe and Aldeburgh, October, 1906

Captain Fyfe-Smythe slumped upon the single remaining chair and picked non-committedly at a deeply embedded shred of steel from the German grenade that had pierced the farmhouse oak table.

The remaining members of his assault team sat upon the floor or lounged exhaustedly about the walls of the small room. The battle was over and they were alive.

Holmes and I stood next to the table. Observing the state of the others, Holmes addressed them.

"Gentlemen, you have my sincere congratulations. You may not realise it but, the action that you have most gloriously achieved this night has done more to ensure the future security of your country, than you may ever realise."

A subaltern entered the room and made his way over to Fyfe-Smythe.

"Excuse me sir. Transport to Colchester is here and awaits your embarcation to barracks," he stated.

Holmes moved to assist the captain as he attempted to rise from the chair. Fyfe-Smythe shook him off.

"I have lost a man tonight, Mr. Holmes," he murmured tiredly. "How do I write to any next of kin and inform them that he died upon a Suffolk beach for a reason that I must never disclose?"

With that, he moved slowly to the farmhouse door, followed by his men.

North Sea, off the coast of Aldeburgh, October, 1906

The explosion had both deafened and stunned his senses.

Sebastian Moran floated, half insensibly within the circular confines of the life buoy.

Slowly his innate sense of preservation flooded his brain. He was alive and needed to get away from his present situation. But where should he go?

The water was cold, very cold.

Although the son of a local inhabitant, Moran had hated

the sea and never learned to swim.

His initial panic in placing himself into an environment wherein he had scant interest or the natural ability to survive, had ceased to trouble him upon the buoyancy afforded by his life buoy.

He was alone and without a single constructive thought as to what he might do now. At least he was afloat.

From his position he could make out a few, dismal, shore based light sources. He decided that his best chance would be to make for these.

Leiston, Suffolk, November, 1906

Currel Daward had risen early that morning, eaten breakfast and bid farewell to his dear wife.

Business had provided an opportunity to visit a local small holding upon which the owner required a quick sale.

The little house itself was of small value, yet the accompanying large barn might be of some interest to a purchaser seeking weatherproof storage.

Having completed his measurements of the house, Currel Daward entered the dusty confines.

Having surveyed the building and about to leave, his attention was drawn to the figure that lay or rather crouched within the far corner of the building.

The man, for the gender of the discovered figure evidenced such, appeared within the final vestiges of collapse and thus, incapable of responsive conversation. However Currel Daward discovered that the other was a gentleman of some standing in the country's capital, who wishing to experience the delights of coastal fishing, had hired a small boat without knowledge of the craft's handling, wandered into the unforgiving seas of the Suffolk coast where his tiny craft had capsized. By the grace of God, his life had been preserved by the vessel's life raft, upon which his drenched and shivering body had reached the coast. Knowing not where to go, he had discovered the barn in which the other had discovered him.

It was in the beneficent nature of the man that Currel Daward, insisted that the stranger accompany him to his house in Leiston where he further insisted that the man eat a hearty meal and accept a change of clothes from his host's own wardrobe and also accept both travel expenses and further moneys for his conveyance to his own lodgings in London.

At, 3 o'clock upon the same day of his deliverance, the stranger caught the train to London and Currel Daward returned to the loving arms of his adoring, yet gossiping spouse.

German Military Headquarters, Zossen, Germany, November, 1906

Having received and understood the communiqué from the *Komet*, von Schiffert finally accepted that his future career was at an end.

His efforts had resulted in abject failure and his Kaiser would never accept any result, other than complete success. What might be his foreseeable future?

Retirement to his estates in East Prussia was not a decision that fell easily upon his shoulders yet, what else might he anticipate?

Every possible situation that might possibly reflect any involvement by his Emperor within the failed operation had been rigorously attended to.

Yet, his continual requests for an audience had been politely denied by unbelievable excuses that His Majesty was otherwise engaged upon such questionable declinations as, a state visit to Munich, a garden party in Koln or, other spurious and unacceptable reasons.

Von Schiffert began to realise that the outcome of his previous actions, might not figure within the Emperor's current thoughts.

Norwich-London express, November, 1906

Seated comfortably within the confines of a first class compartment, Sebastian Moran stretched his legs to rest upon the opposite bench seat. He felt good.

In fact, he felt very satisfied.

A return to Germany was definitely out of the question but, there was a selection of others who might value the work that he was most able to provide. The minor states of the Balkans flashed across his distorted mind. They were always seeking a catalyst such as himself to stir up revolution.

He stood up and adjusted his recently borrowed clothes. They very nearly fit.

He looked at the eye level mirror within the compartment and smiled wickedly.

All was possible but now, he wanted a cup of tea and a bun.

Humming softly to himself, he made his way down the corridor to the restaurant car.

Borgen Club, Tiergarten Alee, Berlin, November, 1906

Von Schiffert was now, more than concerned.

It had been over two weeks since he had been informed that the plan had failed, yet he had received no summons from the Kaiser.

His worry had caused his consumption of more than he was used to at the small private club that he and certain senior officers favoured.

He was mentally concerned and upon realising his unusual, alcoholic state, decided to leave the premises earlier than he normally did.

The exceptionally mild day followed by the chill of an October night had caused a dense, impenetrable fog that swirled in dark clouds within the Berlin streets. It was thus that von Schiffert initially failed to notice the approach of the figure until his right leg was tripped and he toppled over to the pavement.

Attempting to stand from a position that he had never before been forced to adopt, he felt a pair of gentle hands upon his throat.

Strangely soft yet powerful fingers sought, delved and found the carotid artery and deeper, into the vagus nerve.

Von Schiffert's birth had taken 4 hours. His death occurred in 4 seconds.

Herbert Kroller gently returned the lifeless body to the pavement, stood up and disappeared into the fog.

Offices of Military Intelligence, Whitehall, November, 1906

Spencer Ewart was in the highest of spirits.

"Well done the both of you!" he exhilarated. "You have saved your country in the moment of its direst peril. Although none but a few will ever know of your positive involvement, I have been asked to extend to you both your government's sincere and grateful thanks."

"What of Moran?" said Holmes. "Has his body been recovered?"

"Not to my current knowledge," replied Spencer Ewart. "Then again, if he were upon the boat when it was hit by the destroyer's shell, I fear that little of him would remain for identification purposes.

"I am a firm believer in the Latin maxim *habeas corpus*," said Holmes drily. "Where there is no body, death cannot be presumed."

The other appeared somewhat flustered at Holmes's continued questioning.

"Come, come, my dear fellow, the man in question is undeniably dead. That's an end to it!"

"Only time will tell." replied Holmes. "Were there any survivors?"

"Two," replied the other. "The first appears to be a French dissident who has no idea for whom he was working and whose only complaint is that he will not now receive the money he was promised."

"And the other?" enquired Holmes.

"We managed to apprehend a young man who claims to be a German born physicist recruited by a section of German Intelligence," replied. "According to our interrogation section, the youth, horrified by the actions that he has experienced, is only too willing to change his allegiance and work for us. We have offered this individual a change of name and the opportunity to work with Signor Marconi to perfect the device so valued by the German agents. I believe that he has willingly agreed to this suggestion. It would appear that all's well that ends well."

"Having definite proof now that this foul action was at the behest of the German government," said Holmes, "what political action does His Majesty's government intend to take?"

"None!" said the other. "Diplomatic relations with Germany are at best fragile at this moment and as their planned operation failed so dismally, it is felt that the current *status quo* between our two nations should be preserved. To all intents and purposes, the events of the last weeks never happened."

"I see," remarked Holmes. He took out his Hunter and studied the time face.

"If our meeting is concluded," he said. "I have to visit an old friend who has lost his pet monkey and seeks my assistance in recovering the same."

Spencer Ewart appeared aghast. "Goodness Holmes!"

he virtually exploded. "You mean to tell me that you also use your undeniable talent to discover the whereabouts of animals?"

Holmes leant across the table. "The gentleman in question is a very old friend of mine who has but little time to live. I could hardly do less."

We both rose to leave but Holmes looked back at the other and smiled wickedly.

"I note that your batman has had little success with that egg stain."

Spencer Ewart looked down upon his jacket then back at Holmes.

"What egg stain?" he cried. "My uniform is as pristine as it was upon the day it was made."

Holmes actually giggled out loud. "My dear Spencer Ewart," he chortled. "For a man in your position, you are most easily led."

For a few moments Spencer Ewart said nothing the, his face creased with laughter. "That is the second time that you have had me, Holmes," he guffawed. "There will not be a third. Of that I do assure you."

We made our way to the door. Suddenly, Spencer Ewart called to us. "Wait a minute! I have forgotten the point of this meeting."

We turned back.

"A person of the highest rank wishes to impart his own thanks for the services you have rendered."

"Do you refer to the Prime Minister?" said Holmes.

"No!" answered the other.

"It is His Majesty the King.

Stadtschloss, Berlin, November, 1906

The Kaiser regarded the small man that knelt before him. For a few seconds, the German emperor relished his position upon the throne he occupied.

"You can assure me that, General von Schiffert is dead?" he began. The other nodded. The Kaiser sighed loudly.

"This news saddens me," he began. "There will have to be a state funeral. The man was one of my senior staff generals. Nothing less will be appropriate."

For another few seconds he looked down upon the other.

"You've performed an excellent service both to me and your country, Herr Kroller," he stated. "Although my public appreciation may not be evidenced for obvious reasons, I have instructed that a town house and its domestic services within the residential district of Potsdam be immediately placed at your disposal."

Kroller said nothing.

The Kaiser continued. "Rest assured my dear Kroller, I may have need of your particular services again."

At this, the Kaiser rose from his seat and in a simple movement of his good hand, dismissed the other.

The German emperor gently tweaked his stiffly tonsured moustache and strutted to the large window that overlooked the magnificent park surrounding his palace. He stared blankly through the polished glass and hummed a lullaby that his mother, Victoria, had learned from her mother, his adored grand Mamma.

His reverie was interrupted by a page who announced

the arrival of General von Schlieffen.

"Admit the general!" ordered the Kaiser.

The man that entered, bore an incredible likeness to Chancellor Bismarck whom the Kaiser had dismissed from office several years earlier. Bald and bewhiskered, he slowly made his way across the room, halted in front of the Kaiser and attempted to click the heels of his highly polished boots, in the required fashion.

"My dear von Schlieffen," said the Kaiser. "Please take a seat."

Von Schlieffen gratefully accepted his emperor's offer.

"I have knowledge of a plan," commented the general.

"What of it?" asked the Kaiser.

Von Schlieffen began.

"I have studied the existing military status of Germany and its European neighbours, my Kaiser," replied von Schlieffen. I am convinced that a situation may occur when a state of war will inevitably exist between this country and at least one of the others. I have therefore prepared a strategy that will ensure our dominance should this event happen."

The Kaiser leant forward.

"Then please explain your thoughts and corresponding actions in more detail, Herr General?"

The Mall, London, November, 1906

The Mall sparkled beneath the bright sun of a November morning.

The air was crisp and tangy, suggesting a sharp winter to follow.

As our carriage passed *the* tree, I searched again for the little bird that had so earlier attracted my attention. It or one of its family was back upon the same branch and filling the chilly air with its sibilant song.

"Whatever are you staring at, Watson?" enquired Holmes.

"It has returned." said I.

"What has?" said Holmes, rather petulantly.

"The little goldfinch that I saw when we were on our way to meet Spencer Ewart," I replied. "It's back."

"Good Lord!" cried Holmes, "we are about to meet with the King and yet, your only concern appears to be with a small, insignificant, feathered creature that has appeared upon a branch where thousands may gather. Really Watson!"

"The presence of the creature, whether it be the same as I originally viewed or just another goldfinch, suggests to my simple mind that England is itself again," I replied defensively.

Holmes groaned audibly.

"My God, Watson!" he mumbled. "Whatever am I to do with you?"

I continued staring at the sparrow but distinctly heard his next words.

"Then again," muttered Holmes, "whatever might I

possibly do without you?"

The man looked at us beneath those memorable hooded eyes that betrayed his royalty.

For a second, the mouth, concealed to a greater extent within the heavy bearded and whiskered features remained still and compressed. Then it visibly relaxed. We had been invited to an audience with the King at Buckingham Palace. Just us and no one else.

"Our late and well-beloved mother has upon several occasions informed us upon the valuable services that you both have provided in the past," said the King.

"The present matter, we are assured by my Prime Minister, has perforce to remain a state secret. Thus, we are unable to reward you with such honours as you deserve."

The King stood up and we followed.

"However," continued the King, "We are able to offer you both your sovereign and our country's abject thanks for your recent activities that have resulted in resolving a situation that might have proved calamitous without your assistance."

"It was our duty," began Holmes but. King Edward waved him aside with a waft of his royal hand.

"Duty, my dear Holmes, is the prerogative of royalty," he began. "Ability and the use of it, is the requirement of any others. You, my dear gentlemen, possess both attributes."

We said nothing.

The King came down to our level.

"We have a small private enclave within these grounds, within which we tend to invite our personal acquaintances," he said. "It is equipped with the most excellent wines, brandies and whiskies and a selection of the most sought after Cuban cigars. It is but a short walk from the palace. Would you care to join us?"

Upon our way out, the King nudged me and winked.

"You know, Watson," he murmured. "The Queen actually hates me smoking but, with a doctor in my presence," and he nudged me again, "what can she really complain upon?"

END

Also from MX Publishing

MX Publishing is the world's largest specialist Sherlock Holmes publisher, with over a hundred titles and fifty authors creating the latest in Sherlock Holmes fiction and non-fiction.

From traditional short stories and novels to travel guides and quiz books, MX Publishing cater for all Holmes fans.

The collection includes leading titles such as _Benedict Cumberbatch In Transition_ and _The Norwood Author_ which won the 2011 Howlett Award (Sherlock Holmes Book of the Year).

MX Publishing also has one of the largest communities of Holmes fans on Facebook with regular contributions from dozens of authors.

www.mxpublishing.com

Also from MX Publishing

Our bestselling books are our short story collections;

'Lost Stories of Sherlock Holmes' , 'The Outstanding Mysteries of Sherlock Holmes', The Papers of Sherlock Holmes Volume 1 and 2, 'Untold Adventures of Sherlock Holmes' (and the sequel 'Studies in Legacy) and 'Sherlock Holmes in Pursuit', 'The Cotswold Werewolf and Other Stories of Sherlock Holmes' – and many more......

www.mxpublishing.com

Also from MX Publishing

"Phil Growick's, 'The Secret Journal of Dr Watson', is an adventure which takes place in the latter part of Holmes and Watson's lives. They are entrusted by HM Government (although not officially) and the King no less to undertake a rescue mission to save the Romanovs, Russia's Royal family from a grisly end at the hand of the Bolsheviks. There is a wealth of detail in the story but not so much as would detract us from the enjoyment of the story. Espionage, counter-espionage, the ace of spies himself, double-agents, double-crossers...all these flit across the pages in a realistic and exciting way. All the characters are extremely well-drawn and Mr Growick, most importantly, does not falter with a very good ear for Holmesian dialogue indeed. Highly recommended. A five-star effort."

The Baker Street Society

www.mxpublishing.com

Also from MX Publishing

The Missing Authors Series

Sherlock Holmes and The Adventure of The Grinning
Cat
Sherlock Holmes and The Nautilus Adventure
Sherlock Holmes and The Round Table Adventure

"Joseph Svec, III is brilliant in entwining two endearing and enduring classics of literature, blending the factual with the fantastical; the playful with the pensive; and the mischievous with the mysterious. We shall, all of us young and old, benefit with a cup of tea, a tranquil afternoon, and a copy of Sherlock Holmes, The Adventure of the Grinning Cat."
Amador County Holmes Hounds Sherlockian Society

Also from MX Publishing

The American Literati Series

The Final Page of Baker Street
The Baron of Brede Place
Seventeen Minutes To Baker Street

"The really amazing thing about this book is the author's ability to call up the 'essence' of both the Baker Street 'digs' of Holmes and Watson as well as that of the 'mean streets' of Marlowe's Los Angeles. Although none of the action takes place in either place, Holmes and Watson share a sense of camaraderie and self-confidence in facing threats and problems that also pervades many of the later tales in the Canon. Following their conversations and banter is a return to Edwardian England and its certainties and hope for the future. This is definitely the world before The Great War."
Philip K Jones

www.mxpublishing.com

Also from MX Publishing

The Detective and The Woman Series

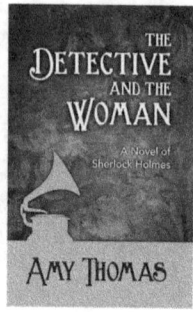  

The Detective and The Woman
The Detective, The Woman and The Winking Tree
The Detective, The Woman and The Silent Hive

"The book is entertaining, puzzling and a lot of fun. I believe the author has hit on the only type of long-term relationship possible for Sherlock Holmes and Irene Adler. The details of the narrative only add force to the romantic defects we expect in both of them and their growth and development are truly marvelous to watch. This is not a love story. Instead, it is a coming-of-age tale starring two of our favorite characters."
Philip K Jones

www.mxpublishing.com

Also from MX Publishing

The Sherlock Holmes and Enoch Hale Series

The Amateur Executioner
The Poisoned Penman
The Egyptian Curse

"The Amateur Executioner: Enoch Hale Meets Sherlock Holmes", the first collaboration between Dan Andriacco and Kieran McMullen, concerns the possibility of a Fenian attack in London. Hale, a native Bostonian, is a reporter for London's Central News Syndicate - where, in 1920, Horace Harker is still a familiar figure, though far from revered. "The Amateur Executioner" takes us into an ambiguous and murky world where right and wrong aren't always distinguishable. I look forward to reading more about Enoch Hale."

Sherlock Holmes Society of London

www.mxpublishing.com

Also from MX Publishing

Sherlock Holmes novellas in verse

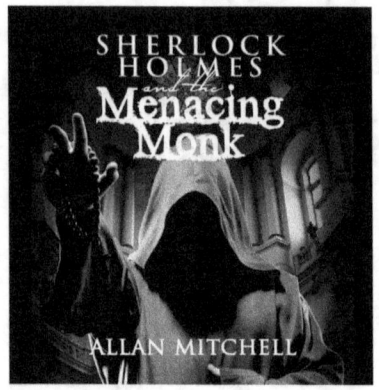

All four novellas
have been
released also in
audio format
with narration
by Steve White

Sherlock Holmes and The Menacing Moors
Sherlock Holmes and The Menacing Metropolis
Sherlock Holmes and The Menacing Melbournian
Sherlock Holmes and The Menacing Monk

"The story is really good and the Herculean effort it must have been to write it all in verse—well, my hat is off to you, Mr. Allan Mitchell! I wouldn't dream of seeing such work get less than five plus stars from me..." **The Raven**

Also from MX Publishing

When the papal apartments are burgled in 1901, Sherlock Holmes is summoned to Rome by Pope Leo XII. After learning from the pontiff that several priceless cameos that could prove compromising to the church, and perhaps determine the future of the newly unified Italy, have been stolen, Holmes is asked to recover them. In a parallel story, Michelangelo, the toast of Rome in 1501 after the unveiling of his Pieta, is commissioned by Pope Alexander VI, the last of the Borgia pontiffs, with creating the cameos that will bedevil Holmes and the papacy four centuries later. For fans of Conan Doyle's immortal detective, the game is always afoot. However, the great detective has never encountered an adversary quite like the one with whom he crosses swords in "The Vatican Cameos.."

"An extravagantly imagined and beautifully written Holmes story" (**Lee Child**, NY Times Bestselling author, Jack Reacher series)

Also from MX Publishing

The Conan Doyle Notes (The Hunt For Jack The Ripper)

"Holmesians have long speculated on the fact that the Ripper murders aren't mentioned in the canon, though the obvious reason is undoubtedly the correct one: even if Conan Doyle had suspected the killer's identity he'd never have considered mentioning it in the context of a fictional entertainment. Ms Madsen's novel equates his silence with that of the dog in the night-time, assuming that Conan Doyle did know who the Ripper was but chose not to say – which, of course, implies that good old stand-by, the government cover-up. It seems unlikely to me that the Ripper was anyone famous or distinguished, but fiction is not fact, and "The Conan Doyle Notes" is a gripping tale, with an intelligent, courageous and very likable protagonist in DD McGil."
The Sherlock Holmes Society of London